RIDING THE EDGE

KTS #1

ELISE FABER

RIDING THE EDGE
BY ELISE FABER

RIDING THE EDGE
Copyright © 2020 Elise Faber
Print ISBN-13: 978-1-946140-84-5
Ebook ISBN-13: 978-1-946140-83-8
Cover Art by Jena Brignola

KTS

PROLOGUE

San Francisco, California, USA
06:34hrs local time

Dan

WEDDING BELLS AND BAKERY SMELLS.

If that didn't encapsulate this day, then I didn't know what did.

But that wasn't the *most* important thing about the day.

I had more work to do.

And it did *not* involve downing more of the delicious confections that were created in this building.

For one, they weren't good for my waistline. I had put on a good five pounds since I'd begun this protection and investigation detail. For another, it was time I remove myself and the complication of KTS from the blissful couple's lives.

Their part in this shitshow was done.

They'd sacrificed, risked their lives, and now they deserved a peaceful future.

Which meant I needed to circle back to work.

I slipped out the back of the bakery on a sigh, relieved this part of the mission was finally complete. I'd only come because my presence at this informal wedding had been requested by two people I respected beyond measure.

Jackson and Molly, the couple I'd been protecting, hadn't gone to a big church or invested in the puffy dress. Not this time.

Today they were just two people in love getting a second chance.

People who had missed their first chance because we couldn't get our shit done. Two people who'd nearly missed their *second* chance because of the same, because KTS had failed them.

Some agent, huh?

"Fuck," I muttered, part of my mind making sure the door closed, the rest scanning the surrounding area for threats. But deep down, I was so damned tired of the guilt, even as a part of me knew it was just part of the job. When I'd been cherry-picked from the FBI a few years before and folded into the private sector, I had already been well-familiar with the failures that were common in this line of work.

Not every case was solved.

Not everyone came out alive.

Not every ending was happy.

I got that. I . . . just hadn't expected to find it so fucking depressing to be working for an agency with a bigger reach, who took on bigger bad guys from around the world.

Because despite the larger budget and greater access to resources, sometimes the bad guys still won.

And the *only* thing I hated more than the bad guys winning was when it was *my* fault.

"I knew you'd be here."

I didn't react. I might feel like a failure when it came to

taking down the Mikhailova clan, but I was damned good at being aware of my surroundings, of keeping myself alive.

So, I knew Laila was there, had slipped out the back door of the bakery, same as me. Knew she'd come to the wedding for the same reason as me—she'd gotten close to the couple, felt the same connection with Molly and Jackson as me.

And we both wanted to see the couple happy.

Because happy didn't happen often enough in this industry.

But just as I knew Laila had emerged from inside, even though I'd hardly made a sound when opening that heavy metal door, I also knew that Ava had come out behind her.

Ava.

Peaches. Humid summer days. Whiskey and lemonade and—

Fuck. *Ava.*

She strode over to me, curves in a compact body, shining brown hair swept up into a ponytail that swung behind her shoulders as she moved, strength and confidence . . . and so many painful memories.

Her eyes looked right through me, minimizing everything that had happened between us two years ago.

Then those eyes narrowed, focused on me, seared straight into my soul.

"We found the hard drives."

A beat as Laila came forward and crossed her arms, expression furious.

"And we know what's on them."

ONE

Dan

I WAS DEAD.

I knew that the moment I saw the shadow shift out of the corner of my eye.

Knew it even as I burst into motion, moving in what would prove to be a vain attempt to avoid a speeding bullet.

Pain exploded in my chest as I dove behind a wall, hitting the ground hard.

My lungs struggled to work, but I clamped down on the gasp of agony before it could escape.

Shot.

Not for the first time. Probably not for the last.

That thought gave me a blip of clarity, allowed me to take a moment to catalog the injury. Blood seeped out of the wound on both my chest and back. The first was a problem. The second gave me hope the bullet had been a through and through.

"Report."

That voice in my ear had the fog that was encroaching on the edges of my vision dissipating. It rolled down my spine like honey, brought the memory of that secret week two years ago to the forefront of my brain.

We'd pretended nothing had happened for two years. Or *Ava* had pretended. We'd gone back to work, and it was like nothing had changed for *her*.

Except, *everything* had changed for me and—

Focus.

"Took one," I gritted out, locking down the pain, the memories. I'd had plenty of practice at that. Inhaling sharply, I pushed to my knees. I wore a bulletproof vest, though, of course, Murphy's Law would dictate the shot had hit one of the few spots on my torso with no protection. "But I have the package and heading to the extraction point."

"Negative," Ava said. "Stay put. I've got eyes on the target."

It went against my every instinct to listen. I might not be the leader of this team, but I'd made it a point to be the first in and the last out when it came to the missions.

But . . . something was *really* wrong here.

This was supposed to be a simple pickup of information.

And within minutes, it had devolved into something that was absolutely FUBAR. Our informant had shown up bleeding, staggering into the abandoned warehouse that was the meeting point. Gunshots had rung out moments later, and I'd covered the informant with my body as I'd yanked him to the side.

But even with that intervention, the man had barely taken two more breaths before he'd gone into the afterlife.

Leaving me to pick through the dead man's pockets like a fucking graverobber for the USB with the files my employer needed.

KTS was a private military operation, unofficially sanctioned by the U.S., British, and German governments, but not technically under the purview of any of them. We operated on the fringes, our edict simple.

Erase the really fucking bad guys.

Which wouldn't have a chance of happening unless the USB in my pocket made it safely to headquarters.

Plus, if I died, I'd never get another chance with Ava.

"Agent?" came the crisp voice. "Stay down. Do you copy?"

I blinked, yanked my mind into focus. It was wandering, shifting to unimportant things because of the injury, the blood loss, the pain. Grinding my teeth and pressing my free hand to the wound on my chest, I hissed out a breath then said, "Copy."

All went quiet.

And I was silently bleeding out on a cold concrete floor.

TWO

Ava

THIS WAS BULLSHIT.

The whole op was a complete and utter disaster.

Starting with the late arrival of our contact—a bleeding and now dead contact—and ending with the agent I was supposed to be covering getting shot. And if I knew anything about Dan, it was that he tended to overestimate his ability and underestimate his injury level.

Not that he wasn't a talented member of the KTS team.

It was just that he was a *man*.

A slice of masculine deliciousness I'd tasted every inch of two years before—which so wasn't the point. Because it wasn't just that we'd scratched an itch together.

I *liked* him. Respected him.

Pretended to hate him when all I wanted to do was dive into his arms and have a repeat of that glorious week.

Dan was a male who didn't subscribe to the notion of the Man Cold, wouldn't be found moping in bed over some sniffles. He was a person I'd seen take serious internal damage and keep going until the mission was complete.

Some might say it was reckless.

And, I supposed, it probably was.

But I was right there with him, had pushed through instances when the circumstances had surpassed dangerous and moved into deadly, ignored times when I should have stopped or retreated. Dan had been there, at my back, had in fact pulled me out of several close scrapes . . . even though I'd hurt him.

I knew I had.

But I'd *had* to. There was no other choice, not with Dan.

He was too good for me to drag him into my special circle of Hell.

Still, that one week in Georgia haunted me.

It had started as a break between missions in the middle of summer, when he'd offered to show me part of the U.S. I hadn't seen before. We'd driven through tiny towns, stopping at Dan's small cabin set on a peach orchard, the air unbearably humid and rainstorms coming out of nowhere, drenching us in sheet after sheet of precipitation. It had stretched into us spending a week there, eating ripe peaches off the trees, juice dripping down our chins, getting drunk on whiskey and lemonade, and learning every inch of each other's bodies.

For a full week, it had been bliss.

And then it had ended when my past had reminded me that I wasn't good for him.

I was seriously fucked up, parts of me permanently broken, never to be reformed, and so . . . I'd made it crystal clear there could be no future.

I'd pretended nothing had changed between us.

Even though *everything* had changed.

After reality struck, I'd rebuffed him at every opportunity, pushed him away until he'd retreated. It hadn't been easy, but I'd perfected locking down every soft feeling. And . . . we worked together. It was either get along, pretend there wasn't anything between us, or move to a different team at KTS.

It was only after I'd threatened the last that he'd stopped pushing.

So, here we were.

On a mission, me pretending so hard to hate him, it almost seemed like reality. Except, of course, for the memories that wouldn't stay locked away, the way my body remembered his, *wanted* him.

"Enough, Ava," I whispered.

He'd saved my ass more than once, so I was going to return the favor. Maybe I wouldn't ever be the type of woman who would hug him or tend to his boo-boos.

But I knew something about loyalty.

How important it was. How much it hurt when it wasn't there.

I might not be a normal woman, had been shattered into too many pieces inside to ever have any hope of that, but I could be a good agent.

And I was a damned good sniper.

No shaking hands. No targets missed.

I sighted. I squeezed the trigger. They went down—

There.

I caught the flicker of movement, trained my sights on the target through my scope—it wouldn't do to take out an innocent —and maybe it should have worried me, how detached I'd become to the killing that I barely gave the thought a considera- tion—and only a cavalier one at that—but I had a job to do that was more important than gentle emotions and civilian worries.

Get out alive.

Get *Dan* out alive.

Get the files back to headquarters.

Movement in the shadows. Closing in on Dan. *Fuck.* I wasn't in a great position myself, had moved to get eyes on him, and now I was potentially exposed.

But my partner in this was a fucking sitting duck.

One that I'd told to stay there.

I had to take care of this.

Kneeling, I rested my rifle on a ledge on the upper story of the abandoned building. It was falling apart, didn't offer much protection. But it was in the shadows, and I had a clear sight line.

I adjusted my glasses, the ones I despised having to wear, but the ones that also made it so I could site the enemy through my scope as he stepped closer to Dan, and my finger went to the trigger of my rifle, rested on the curved piece of metal.

A glint as the man extracted a weapon.

Another layer of FUBAR because I knew there were more bad guys around but hadn't been able to pinpoint their locations.

The man took another step, and—

No more time.

Ready. Set. Squeezing the trigger slowly and steadily so as not to be surprised by the gun firing.

Pop.

"Move," I hissed to myself the second the bullet was away.

My shot hit its target, and the man collapsed. But it was dark, and the moment I'd taken the shot, the flash of light emanating from the barrel of my rifle meant my position was compromised.

Pop. Pop. Pop.

The bullets collided with the wall behind me, ricocheting

off the steel siding, sending tiny arrows of metal exploding into the air.

One sliced across my cheek, a slight burn of pain I barely felt.

Because I was flying.

Jumping down from my perch, landing on the ground in a crouch that both saved my knees from injury and made me a smaller target. Footsteps clattered on the concrete, closing in on me, but I'd spent years training for exactly these kinds of missions. I burst into movement, my rifle spun to rest on my back, a knife from the holster strapped to my calf already in my hand, and burst to my feet, erupting in a flurry of violence toward the first enemy to approach.

Not expecting a frontal attack, he stumbled back a step before engaging me in hand-to-hand combat.

But I'd already taken advantage of the opening my assault had given me.

A precise slice to the thigh had the man dropping to his knees. A strike to the back of his head knocked him unconscious.

I heard rather than saw him collapse because I was still moving.

Thunk.

My knife sunk into a throat as I dodged a blow from the left, reaching behind me at the same time and getting off two quick shots that bought me some time and space to assess.

Three more targets, and who the fuck knew if there were more in the warehouse. One thing was absolutely clear.

I needed to *move.*

I struck out—kicked and jabbed as frequently as I blocked and dodged.

And within thirty seconds, I'd dispatched the first two. But I struggled with the third, who was bigger and stronger and too damned quick. A blow to my ribs had me biting back a gasp of pain, and another to my cheek was less glancing than bruise-inducing.

It wasn't, however, consciousness-stealing as I'd managed to dart back, to prevent it from hitting my temple.

My glasses clattered to the concrete, but luckily they were for distance rather than up close, so I kicked them to the side and retreated a few steps. Then ribs burning, breaths coming in controlled bursts, I gripped my rifle like a baseball bat and treated my pride and joy as I had always promised I wouldn't . . .

"Sorry, Luna," I apologized to my steadfast companion.

Then I smashed the rifle against my opponent's temple.

He collapsed to the ground, tipping over and hitting the concrete like a tree dropping to the forest floor, rapidly and with a jarring noise. Sliding my weapon back over my shoulder, I took stock of my surroundings.

Stillness surrounded us, making my near-silent movements seem gunshot loud in the space, but I knew it wouldn't be quiet for long.

Even now, I could hear the slight buzz of the earpieces the men had worn, their compatriots checking in on their fallen companions. Clearly, they wouldn't get a response, which meant it was likely Dan and I wouldn't be alone in the warehouse for long.

If they'd sent a crew to capture the files our source had brought—hell, if they'd cared enough to try (and succeed) in killing the source, they wouldn't give up easily.

They were coming. And they were coming soon.

So . . . it was time to go.

I picked up my glasses, ran over to where Dan was, jumped over the wall, and opened my mouth—

Click.

"Stop fucking around," I hissed, glaring at Dan even as I

assessed him for injuries. He dropped the gun to his side, fumbled to secure it back in his holster, and I could see that blood had soaked through his shirt, making the black fabric stick to his skin. Just took one? Ha. The man was going to bleed out without help.

"Tie this for me," he muttered, tearing open a field bandage from the kit we all had stored in our boots while on missions. It was hidden in the tongue of our footwear and coated with a special KTS-patented substance that would help with clotting.

He fumbled, starting to wrap it around the wound.

I grabbed the strip of material around his torso, binding it tightly and ignoring his grunt of pain. One, because it needed to be tight or he was going to bleed out on the floor. Two, we didn't have time for me to dawdle over tying a delicate bow.

Three, I wasn't exactly known for my bedside manner.

There wasn't *anything* soft or sweet or gentle about me. Dan had witnessed that firsthand, so there was no need to sugarcoat anything.

Hard lines and barbed wire, bullets instead of Band-Aids, sharp words rather than kissed knees.

I'd never had any soft in my life, and at this point I didn't *want* it.

Soft was useless. Hard could protect, could strike out before the hurt came. Hard was—

Booted feet on concrete.

Fuck.

I tied off the knot, hitched my shoulder under Dan's, and started to heave him to his feet. But I'd barely begun to use my strength and he was up, looking far steadier than a man who'd just taken a bullet should.

He grabbed his pack, nodded toward the shadows. "Let's go."

Respect curled through me.

Unfortunately, as my gaze drifted to the wounded man's ass, stayed there for a heartbeat too long, it wasn't the *only* thing curling through me.

Bullets, barbed wire, and . . .

A hard on for one Dan Plantain.

One I'd had for too many years to count.

Fuck.

THREE

KTS Satellite Headquarters
Munich, Germany
01:33hrs local time

Dan

I HISSED at the burn of antiseptic trailing over my skin.

"This'll be two weeks light duty," Olive said.

My spine stiffened, an argument on the tip of my tongue.

"At minimum."

Now, the argument escaped. Or at least one syllable before I was shut down. "I—"

"Nope," Laila said, glancing up from the computer. "The first rule of KTS is no arguing with the doctor who's patching up your ass. We only have one doc on the team and don't want her to abandon us."

Olive snorted. "You guys are the cool team," she said. "I could never abandon you."

"Shh," Laila replied. "It's the only way I have to keep this one in check. Or to not get any grand ideas about going off on his own."

I huffed. "I don't need the drama of running my own team all the time. It's bad enough when I have to do it on occasion."

The vast majority of KTS was broken up into teams of five to ten agents, each usually working as separate units. Sometimes we grouped up, if our missions overlapped, or reorganized briefly if a certain subset of skills was needed for a particular task. But for the most part, we each stayed with our own team, receiving an assignment and seeing it through to the end.

For the past two years, Laila's team had been focusing on the Russian mob, and more specifically, focusing on one clan, which was heading what our team suspected was one of the largest human trafficking rings in the world.

There was a special place in Hell for people who harmed innocents.

And, one could hope, an even *more* special place for those who made their living by selling men, women, and children.

"I thought the first rule of KTS was to get the bad guys," I said, clenching my jaw when a wave of pain washed over me as Olive poked and prodded at the wound on my back.

"Wrong," Laila said. "That's, at minimum, rule three."

"What's rule two?" I gritted, trying to keep my voice even as white-hot agony radiated through me.

"Rule two is to never argue with your team leader."

"Sure it—" I broke off, biting back a curse when Olive did something that rained fire down my spine. Sweat beaded on my forehead, and my head went fuzzy. But I still didn't want to be sidelined for fourteen fucking days. I'd had worse injuries, and the bad guys were still out there.

Starting with the ones who'd killed our source.

"Two weeks light duty," Olive repeated. "And if you argue, I'll make it three."

I made a face, trying to keep my voice even. "You know my mom used to use that same threat with me," I gritted.

"Did it work?"

Yes. Yes, it had.

But I didn't admit that aloud. Instead, I focused on keeping still when I was really, *really* done with all the wound tending. Slap a Band-Aid on. Or hell, just rub some dirt in it and be done.

Fucking doctors.

Wanted to be all sanitary and shit.

But since Olive didn't appear to intend to stop the doctoring anytime soon, I shut up and held still, my gaze moving from Laila, who was transferring files from the USB onto KTS's servers, to Ava.

Tiny. Curvy.

Strong as hell. A woman who was a foot shorter than me and still could easily knock me to my ass, *and* I knew most of her dirty tricks.

But she always seemed to have more dirty tricks.

When I'd asked her about those tricks a week ago, while we'd been preparing for this mission, asked her how she'd become so adept at hand-to-hand combat, her pale brown eyes had filled with pain.

Such pain that I'd actually stepped toward her, wanting to take her into my arms, to hold her close and stroke a hand up and down her spine, promising that everything would be okay. I'd held her once, and it had soothed every ache inside me. But we'd been pretending since then—to only be teammates, that we had not been intimate for a week, that we hadn't shared all of what we'd shared.

Glorious, physical satisfaction.

But so much more than that.

Or at least *I'd* thought it was more.

I'd shared. I'd opened up. And it was only later, after we'd come back to headquarters, when the job was starting up again and she'd gone back to being distant, that I'd realized what she hadn't given.

I'd told her about growing up with apathetic parents, how that used to make me angry until I'd traveled around the world and seen so many other places. That was before I'd realized how much I'd had—a roof over my head, parents who didn't have to choose between food and paying the electricity bill. Were they a little out of touch? Certainly. Did I have a closer relationship with my best friend's mom rather than my own? Also, yes. Did I speak to my sister far more than either of them? Yes.

But I'd had a *safe* childhood.

And that was more than what most of the people we helped could say.

I also thought it was more than Ava must have had. Because the shadows in her eyes were reminiscent of those in so many of the people we saved.

But I couldn't know for sure.

Because of what she didn't give.

I knew nothing of her parents or how she'd grown up. I knew she appreciated good food, could eat a half-dozen peaches without getting sick, and could hold her whiskey but preferred it laced with lemonade.

I knew she giggled when she was buzzed, and I loved the sound, wanted to hear the quiet, unencumbered laughter all the time.

I knew that she was quiet but whip-smart and with a razor-sharp wit.

I knew she could take out a target at twelve hundred meters, that she could knock me to the mat as easily, that she would and *had* killed to protect.

I knew she was tough and a fighter and very skilled.

But I hadn't even *begun* to know what made those shadows appear in her eyes at the gym a week before. She hadn't let me in that deep during that week and had deliberately kept her distance afterward.

And the longing to know her, to understand her past, her future, her worries and fears and hopes and dreams had never gone away.

ON THAT MAT A WEEK AGO, with me fighting the urge to take her into my arms, Ava must have realized she'd given away something of what was beneath those walls—that she wasn't merely the self-assured, confident yet distant agent she appeared to be to the rest of the team.

That she felt, and felt deep.

Except, I'd only caught a glimpse of those deep feelings before she'd shut down again, those pale brown eyes hardening . . . and then she'd taken me to my ass all over again.

Needless to say, I hadn't been in any position to hand out hugs.

And the moment had passed.

We'd continued with our session—fighting hard enough and with enough intensity to be realistic practice, but not with the intention of wanting to hurt each other. Still, by the end, we'd been breathing rapidly, sweat sheeting our bodies, and each left with more than a few bruises.

I'd also been left with an ache.

To soothe her hurts—because I wasn't a total asshole. But also to get inside the walls—because Ava was fascinating to me —and, fine, I might be a *partial* asshole—because I'd also been desperate to get in her pants again.

From the moment I had laid eyes on her, I'd been enthralled by the juxtaposition that was Ava.

Small, but mighty. Curvy, yet lithely muscled and graceful on her feet. Tiny, but able to take down targets twice her size. Glasses-wearing, yet the most talented sniper at KTS. Hard, so damned hard and impenetrable and unfeeling on the outside.

But I'd caught those glimpses of soft, of vulnerable.

Contradictions.

She was full of them.

Hence, my fascination.

And presently, the object of that fascination was propping up a wall opposite me.

Glaring at me.

As though she were thinking, how dare I have the audacity to get shot on her watch. I might have been affronted—it wasn't like I'd been *intending* to get shot—except that Olive decided at that same moment to pull some Nurse Ratched bullshit with the exit wound on my back.

"Fuck," I hissed, trying not to move even as it felt like she was digging her fingers into the injury.

"What'd you do?" Olive asked, not stopping, even when I squirmed. Her question was half-distracted, and I'd have given her my collection of dumbass yo-yos I'd started accruing in elementary school if she would only *just stop.*

"What do you mean?" I asked, sweat dripping down my temples.

A beat, her voice now completely distracted as she tugged hard on something. I bit back another curse, heard a plink as whatever she'd pulled from my back landed in the metal pan at her side. "It looks like you rolled around in gravel."

"That's . . . uh—" The edges of my vision went dark, and I blinked, rapidly, trying to clear it. ". . . basically what I—" I wavered, feeling my body lean forward, even as I could do nothing to stop it. "The floor was dirty and—"

A firm grip on my uninjured shoulder prevented me from faceplanting.

And finally, Olive stopped jabbing at me. "Too much?"

I opened my mouth to tell her I was fine, but Ava beat me to the punch. "Yes, Ollie. It's too much."

"I'm—" I began.

Olive didn't argue with me or say anything further. Instead, I felt a prick, the slight sting of morphine hitting my system, and the pain immediately edged back.

"Thanks," I murmured, giving in that I'd needed the relief, even as my eyes drifted to Ava's.

She continued to hold on to me, fingers gripping my shoulder firmly. It was the most innocuous contact, and paired with a bone-deep ache across my chest and back, I knew I shouldn't be so aware of it, shouldn't be feeling it so intensely, as though those fingers were reaching into my soul and holding me in place.

And *that* was the morphine talking.

She shifted slightly, her fingers brushing along the bare skin of my arm. *Her* skin wasn't silken, or at least not the skin on her hands. I'd felt silken skin in other places, but that covering her fingers and palm was calloused and work-worn, slightly rough against the back of my biceps.

Hers were the hands of action, of a woman who worked hard and put her life on the line at regular intervals.

I fucking loved her hands.

I wanted them to stay on my skin. No, I wanted her hand to drift lower. Or better, to gesture Laila and Olive out of the room and to let *both* of her hands do some investigating.

Further that, if I were making a list of all the things I was wanting, I wanted to not be wounded, to be back at my cabin in Georgia, for her to be touching me because she'd decided to let me into those walls and because she wanted me just as much as I wanted her.

That she wanted my body. *No.* That she wanted more. To see inside me. To allow me to help her carry every old hurt, every painful memory. Fuck, I'd take her just wanting my body, because at least I would have part of her again.

Even if it was a small part. Even if it was the only—

Another tug, another pulse of pain had me jumping.

"Sorry," Olive said. "I'm almost done."

My list of wants dissipated as I swallowed hard, my stomach churning, the black intruding on the edges of my vision again. Fuzziness intruded on my thoughts, my tongue feeling thick and furry, my fingertips tingling. I found it suddenly difficult to make my lips form words as a pleasant floating feeling descended through me.

"You're not going to yak, are you?" Ava's question made me blink rapidly, struggling to focus.

But then that focus narrowed to her, to her fingers on my skin, to her pretty brown hair that was the color of . . . "Mud," I said, my mouth feeling like it was packed with cotton.

"Mud?" she asked.

I nodded, felt my head spin in the process, and reached up to press at my temples. Maybe that would stop the whirling.

"What's mud?" she pressed.

More blinking. More temple pressing. "What?"

A sigh. "Dan, what's the deal with the mud?"

"Your hair," I said. "It's so pretty—"

Ava's eyes drifted over my shoulder. "How much morphine did you give him?"

"Too much, apparently," Olive said. "He never takes the stuff. I formulated the dose for his weight."

"Light bones," I told them.

"What?" they both asked.

"I'm a light bones."

"Lightweight," Ava said. "I think you mean lightweight."

"Yes, *that*." I nodded again, and it was really hard to get my head back up. "I'm a lightweight, and your hair is the color of mud, and it's so pretty, and—"

Ava's gaze darted back to mine.

"—and I want to touch it."

Her eyes widened, lips parting.

And I passed out.

FOUR

Ava

HOLDING the hulking mass of muscle against me so he wouldn't tumble off the table and hit the tile floor, I turned my head toward Laila and lifted a brow.

"Mud?"

My friend, and perhaps the single person on the planet who knew why I hid my emotions behind thick, protective walls, grinned. "But it's *so* pretty."

"Shut up, you," I muttered.

Laila giggled and glanced back at the computer screen, where she was going through the USB we'd recovered. The files had already been encrypted and sent to KTS's main headquarters, where they would be gone over with a fine-tooth comb by a team that specialized in this kind of data. But we wouldn't be good agents if we just sent off intel without learning every bit of information we could. Each agent had some technical capabilities, and while we might not be able to compete with the tech team on all levels, we could hold our own. Plus, we had been trained to be nosy, to squeeze all of the juice out of the proverbial orange, to turn the puzzle over and over and *over* until it was solved. So, it wasn't exactly a surprise that we'd be diving deep into the data.

There was a chain of command, of course, which was why the files had been sent off, and why Laila would be leaving in the next few days or so with the hard copy of the data to take back to headquarters. She would personally meet with the tech team while she was there.

The difference between KTS and other agencies was that while their agents followed the chain of command, we also worked outside of it. Laila's team's directive was to take down a part of the Russian mob—the Mikhailova clan—and we wouldn't stop until that was done. For that reason, we didn't leave the data-combing solely to our techs, just as our techs didn't spend all their time chained to their desks.

Every agent had skills in combat, in hacking, in compartmentalizing and analyzing information to look for patterns and trends and anomalies.

The most obvious of which was why our source, whose meeting had been set up under the most careful conditions—coded message, untraceable cell phone, a location that was chosen and shared at the last minute—wound up with a bullet in his chest.

Two men. Two bullets. Two chests.

The only difference between the men was that one of the bullets had entered two inches higher, and thus mortality hadn't been guaranteed.

Thankfully, the right man had lived.

My stomach clenched, the thought circling through my

mind and filling me with guilt. Guilt because I couldn't summon up more than a bit of disappointment that our source hadn't made it out alive. And . . . more guilt because even if Dan *hadn't* made it out alive, I would have compartmentalized his loss away and moved on.

Which just reinforced the notion that I was broken.

Reducing the man I'd worked side-by-side with to two inches.

And not even in a dirty joke sense.

But that was just it.

I was so messed up inside that I couldn't have a normal relationship with a man. I couldn't *trust* a man. Not now. Not ever.

I had accepted that long ago.

I might scratch an itch on occasion, but before my slip-up two years before, I had always picked men who weren't . . . well, not like Dan.

Not dangerous or smart or able to peek over walls. Or, hell, he was stubborn enough to barrel through the concrete and brick and barbed wire. And he *would* barrel through, that was for damn sure. I saw the way he still looked at me, knew he'd be back in my pants if I gave him the barest indication it was what I wanted. He should be disgusted, but somehow, he wasn't. He'd never lost his temper, even after I'd pushed him away in the most abrupt manner, and he'd always treated me with respect and kindness.

But I didn't want him. That itch had been scratched. Our time was done.

Liar.

Okay fine, my vagina would be happy to get up close and personal with his cock again, but the rest of me—my brain, my sense of self-preservation, and my sanity—knew that I could never let anyone like Dan get close.

He saw too much. He was too good.

And he would *want* too much.

But more than anything else, he deserved so much more than me and my fucked-up past. I wasn't capable of giving a man like Dan what he needed and—

This was why I couldn't keep doing this. I couldn't function and do my job if I was so focused on my childhood, on what brought me to KTS, on the fucking black hole encased in barbed wire and concrete inside me. I needed to be cold and shut down, to not feel or remember anything, to think of only the next mission, the next job, the person I could save to make amends.

Enough.

Fuck, just enough.

Sighing, I glanced over Dan's shoulder again and met Olive's gaze. "He's heavier than he looks," I said. "You almost done?"

The doctor snorted. "You're the strongest person I know, Ava," she said, her eyes dropping back to where her hands were working. "But, for the record, I am almost done. I'll just slap a bandage on, and we'll call it good."

"Is that what you call what you're doing?" I asked dryly. "Slapping things around back there?"

Laila snorted.

"Pretty much," Olive muttered with another plink into the pan next to her, another piece of debris she'd pulled from the bullet wound hitting the bottom of the metal container. There had been far too many of them for my comfort. A rapid *plink-plink-plink* while Dan had grown progressively paler.

And I'd been the only one to notice.

Which was a fact I was deliberately ignoring.

Because if I *didn't* ignore it, if I looked too closely and admitted—even only to myself—that I might be too interested in Dan, might possibly care for him more than a fellow agent, I would be vulnerable. There was a risk if I looked into the razed organ that was my heart, I might see him as a friend . . . or worse, as a *man*.

And that could *not* be.

I knew it just as I knew the sky was blue.

The mere thought made my skin itchy and tight, like hives were just beneath the surface, readying themselves to erupt, and I felt my throat threaten to close as though I'd eaten a piece of cantaloupe—to which I was allergic. I had to force myself to breathe slowly, to not let go of Dan and sprint from the room.

Because no one could see.

He couldn't see.

Well, at least the last was easy to prevent, considering he was unconscious.

"Okay," Olive said, as I tempered the panic inside me. "Lay him down. I'll double-check the bandage on his chest is good to go and then let him—and you—rest."

Shifting him back with a nod, I knew I'd shower first. I was sweaty and dusty and covered in grime, and normally I would have already gone to clean up, but part of me hadn't been able to leave the room, not until I'd seen my partner from the mission was okay.

Simple agent-to-agent concern.

Yup. That was it.

That was the *only* reason—

My eyes met Laila's, and it was as if my friend had seen right into my mind and was cherry-picking my thoughts.

And her pale blue eyes seemed to shout, "Liar!"

Maybe I *was* a liar. But also, maybe that was the only way to get through life unscathed and safe and—

Fuck. Shower. Shut-eye. Then I'd be more like myself.

After Olive had moved the pan and leftover supplies, I carefully tilted Dan back until he was safely resting on the bed. A *click* had the side rail sliding into place and ensuring that he wouldn't be doing any more diving from or over objects, and thus disturbing the treatment he'd just received.

The urge to flee was strong, but I forced myself to close the distance between me and Laila, to act like a responsible agent.

"What do you see?" I asked.

"Fucking gibberish," Laila muttered. "None of this adds up. This isn't like the hard drives we recovered back in San Francisco. Those held copies of bank transfers and statements and accounts and showed the Mikhailova clan in league with prime ministers, arms dealers, several international policing agencies. That was good. We're taking down really awful people in power, but—" She sighed and leaned back in the chair. "I don't get why the source was so determined to meet. Nothing on here seems the least bit connected with them, nor does it seemed to be linked with the trafficking the higher-ups want us to investigate. It's all just . . . inventory and invoices."

I bent and studied the screen sitting on the desk. This, like all other satellite headquarters KTS had located around the world, was a formidable bunker. The entrance was hidden behind several layers of the most secure and technologically advanced protection KTS could provide, as well as staffed by a rotation of agents conducting business in this part of the world. But once beyond all of those walls and keypads and hidden doors with DNA scans, it was reminiscent of our home base in the northeast of England. Narrow bland halls, rooms lined up along either side. Most were sleeping quarters, each with a simple bathroom attached. But each satellite location also had a mess hall, an infirmary, and a technology center.

Laila, in this case, had opted to use the computer in the infirmary.

Mostly because she and Olive were good friends and had wanted to bullshit as they both worked, but also probably because she wanted to pester me.

Not that I minded. Laila had brought me to KTS, had helped me when I had no one else. There was a bond there, one that couldn't be broken, not even by the black hole inside me.

"What kind of inventory?" I asked.

Laila sighed, her blond ponytail flipping over her shoulder as she turned. "That's just it. The inventory on this is for produce." She pointed at the screen. "All lettuce— cabbage, butter, romaine, iceberg, even fucking arugula. More varieties than I even knew existed, and they're all there."

Weird.

I leaned close, read the columns and saw that sure enough, they were sorted by lettuce variety, and each variety was broken up into shipments. So many that my mind spun and my already tired brain blanked. I straightened, pushed up my glasses, and sighed. "Can you make me a copy before you go? I'll dive into it once I've had some sleep."

Laila grinned and handed me a flash drive. "Gotcha covered. Get some shut-eye."

I nodded, headed for the door, pausing when Laila called, "Hey, Av?"

I stopped and turned back. "Yeah?"

"Don't forget to wash that beautiful muddy hair."

Olive snorted, even as Laila burst into obnoxious laughter. I snagged a towel by the door, balled it up, and launched it at my friend.

"You're hilarious," I muttered.

Laila caught the towel. "And you're *so* pretty." A beat. "And muddy."

For fuck's sake, I wouldn't be living that down anytime soon.

FIVE

KTS Satellite Headquarters
Munich, Germany
14:22hrs local time

Dan

I WOKE as I always did—suddenly and with absolute stillness, mind absolutely clear and senses taking stock of my surroundings.

The room was quiet but not empty. I could feel the imprint of someone to my right. The person wasn't moving or making noise, but I could sense their presence, feel the underlying human aura radiating across the room to prickle my nerves. Inhaling slowly, I caught the scent of disinfectant and of some-thing sweet, almost fruity—

Ava.

Lids flying open, my gaze narrowed in on her.

She was sitting at the desk in the corner of the room, her wet hair slicked back into a ponytail that had dampened a U-shape on the back of her T-shirt. She was focused on the computer screen, the light from the monitor highlighting the gentle slope of her nape, the slender build of her shoulders. Fuck, I wanted to be able to stroke those soft, curving lines with my fingers, to trace them with my tongue. I was desperate to have permission to touch her, not just during a sparring session or for simple work purposes. I ached to touch her like a man would touch the woman he *needed* with every fiber of his being.

But she didn't want that.

So I didn't.

Biting back a sigh, I tore my eyes from her and forced myself to scan the remainder of the room. As I'd sensed initially, it was empty except for me and Ava. The tray of tools, the cabinets along one wall, the hand sanitizer mounted by the door all confirmed that I was still in the infirmary.

Silently, I propped my elbows beneath myself, readied to push up.

"Slowly," Ava murmured, not turning from the screen. "Olive said you're likely to be nauseous after the morphine."

I didn't startle. There was a reason I preferred to have Ava at my back. She was a damned good agent, so there was no surprise she'd sensed me using the same skills she'd honed over the years.

Of course, agent skills didn't explain why I'd known deep-down it was Ava before I'd even opened my eyes.

That was something inexplicable.

That was the invisible string tying us together. The one that had been stitched into my soul from the moment I'd met her and had only strengthened over the years.

When I didn't respond, she spun slowly in her chair. "You going to pass out again?"

Shaking my head, I pushed up. Slowly, because while I might be a stubborn pain in the ass in most situations, I wasn't one to disregard sound advice when it came my way. And since my head was spinning and my mouth felt like some mythical creature had died inside it and was desperate to escape, Poltergeist-style, I inched up until I was in a seated position.

"No," I said, once I'd made it. "What did Olive give me? Elephant tranquilizers?"

One side of her mouth hitched up. "Apparently, you're a light bone."

My brows drew down. "What—? *Oh*," I added, the memories pouring back in. Light bone. Lightweight. Pretty hair. *Mud*.

She grinned, and it was such a rare gift that I felt my lungs momentarily freeze.

"Damn," I said, cheeks feeling a bit hot, but knowing there was nothing to be done for it. "High, medication-buzzed Dan doesn't have any game."

"No, he doesn't." She shook her head, turned back to the screen. "Laila has threatened to change my call sign to Mud."

I snorted.

"It's not funny."

I shifted so I could rest my feet on the floor. "It's pretty funny."

"Not so much," she said, typing something on the keyboard. "Though *your* new name is hilarious as far as I'm concerned."

Oh shit.

My stomach sank. "What are you talking about?"

"Come in, Boner."

"Fuck no," I said, carefully standing . . . and immediately wavering so much that I leaned my ass back against the mattress.

"You know the rules," she said. "You don't make the nicknames, you just—"

"—live with them," I finished. "Yeah, yeah. I know."

Cool.

From Wolf to Boner.

The chair squeaked as she turned to face me, and though she wasn't smiling any longer, her expression serious as she studied me standing—okay, more propped up by the bed than actually standing on my own—I could see amusement still dancing in her eyes. She stood and crossed over to me, stopping a foot away, near enough for me to smell her shampoo, the fruity scent I'd come to associate with her.

Fruit and ice.

Sweet and vulnerable and so fucking cold.

But there wasn't frost on her face now.

"How's the wound?" she asked.

I shrugged before I could stop myself then had to bite back a curse because *fuck* that hurt. "Fine," I said when I could speak evenly.

She snorted. "Not fine. Hence the reason for two weeks of light duty."

I groaned but didn't deny that Ava was right. If I could barely stand upright, hardly move my body without fiery pain shooting through my nerves, then it wasn't like I was up to taking down bad guys.

Fuck, it had been a long time since I'd been shot.

The last time Brit had nearly lost her shit.

Speaking of which, maybe I should fly home to San Francisco and visit my sister. It had been too long since I'd seen her, and if I had to be cooling my heels for a couple of weeks—

Yeah, no, dumbass.

I'd wait until I didn't have two healing bullet wounds—one on my chest, one on my back—in my body. My sister had freaked when I'd shown up with one extra hole; the last thing I needed to do was mess up her season by showing up with two.

Not to mention, sitting cooped up on a plane for twelve hours didn't exactly seem like fun at the moment.

"Have you gotten any rest?" I asked.

"Yeah, I crashed after Olive stitched you up. Slept almost ten hours." A shrug. "Woke up. Showered. Ate. Now work."

Considering we'd mobilized at the last minute for the retrieval, both of us catching barely an hour on the plane, and the strain of being ambushed, me getting shot, then trying to get to the rendezvous point unseen, I was half-surprised we both hadn't slept longer.

But the mission wasn't complete.

So maybe half-surprised was too much.

"What was on the file?"

"Nothing I can make sense of yet. Everyone's working on it. I'll make sure you get a copy." She pulled out her phone, tapped the screen. "I just pinged Olive. She wanted to check you over one last time before she and Laila fly back to England."

"I'm fine."

Fine being a relative term.

One at the moment that meant I was conscious and standing.

"You're currently sequestered with no fewer than three extremely stubborn women, one of whom is in charge of our team's medical care, another who is our team leader, and me, who may be the most stubborn of them all," she said. "Do you honestly think you're going to win this argument?"

My only answer was to make a face.

"Exactly," she said. A moment later, her cell buzzed, and she glanced up at me. "Olive will be here in a few."

"Great," I grumbled.

"It's not so bad."

"You're not the one with Boner as a call sign."

She giggled, and I felt a bit of the misery leave me.

Her amusement filled me with joy. Not *all* of me, since I was feeling very pouty about the forced downtime—even though I understood it was necessary—*and* the call sign.

"I might be able to convince them to stick with Wolf."

"How?"

"You'll refuse to use Mud."

I nodded gravely, knowing she was letting me off the hook for my very unsmooth compliments while high on morphine. It wasn't an offer I was going to squander. "Deal."

One half of her mouth curved up. "You know, you're lucky to only have two weeks of light duty. Olive could have easily grounded you for a month or more," she pointed out. "It's better to just take the time to rest, heal up, and be ready to go so she won't need to extend it."

"Don't try to tell me you wouldn't be as miserable about sitting on your ass as I am," I muttered. "We don't get into this job for R&R."

KTS agents weren't known for our relaxed, laid-back attitudes. In fact, if there were a greater subset of Type A personalities anywhere else in the world, then I had yet to find it.

"It's not so bad."

I'd opened my mouth to argue—the idea of doing nothing for weeks on end was worse than bad—then stopped. Because Ava hadn't left the moment I'd awoken. Because she'd come into the infirmary to work, even though she could have chosen any other computer at the base.

Further that, she'd stayed and was talking with me.

Since the week we'd spent together two years before, I could count on one hand the number of times she'd done that, how often she'd just hung out and shot the shit with me.

Hell, I could count it on *one* finger.

Of course, Ava was probably here because I was wounded and at risk of passing out again and Olive had assigned her to make sure I didn't crack open my head on the floor. The doctor was nothing if not practical, and she didn't appreciate treating a patient twice—"once for an injury and twice for stupid."

Yes, that was a direct quote.

Yes, she had the actual T-shirt with the quote emblazoned on the front.

But I digress. For whatever reason, Ava was here, talking to me, and I was soaking up every second. Feeding my addiction, desperate to grasp on to any way to strengthen that thread connecting me to her.

Her eyes danced. "I can hear you thinking, '*It really is that bad, Ava.*'"

"What?"

She laughed, and I felt that husky sound deep in my heart. "I believe we've already established that you and the word 'rest' don't really go hand-in-hand."

I barely heard her words, I was so struck by her laugh.

I hadn't heard it in two long-ass years.

And—

If you want her to ever hang around and laugh and talk to you again, dumbass, focus and say something charming.

The mental voice was Brit's.

Namely, because my sister had been giving me shit from the moment she'd emerged from the womb.

And also because she was normally right.

As she was in this case.

"Thanks for saving my ass," I told Ava, giving in to the fatigue washing over me and sitting down on the bed. "I wouldn't have made it out of there without you."

"You've saved my ass more than once." A shrug, her expression cooling, and I had the distinct impression that I'd said both the right and the wrong thing. She didn't like it when people thanked her for simply doing her job, I knew. But I also understood that she took pride in her work and wouldn't entirely hate having me, as a colleague, compliment her on her skills.

"How many did you take out?" I asked.

Another shrug. "Just four."

I grinned. Only Ava would say *just* four. "How many shots?"

The tension left her shoulders, and she perched onto the bed next to me. "One."

"Ah," I said, trying to pretend that having her so close was no big deal. "You showed off your trickiness on the others."

She rolled her eyes. "It's not trickiness. It's skill."

"I'll remember that next time you take me to the ground."

A ghost of a smile. "I—"

The door opened, and she jumped, hopping to her feet, her gaze zeroing in on the person—on Olive—entering. Since I'd done the same—albeit with less hopping and jumping—I didn't laugh at her reaction.

I was aware, however, that it looked bad for both of us for Ava to be jumping away from me when Olive came in.

How did I know this, one might ask?

Because Olive's smug expression and raised eyebrow were impossible to miss.

The words, "It's not what you think" were on the tip of my tongue, but since saying *that* would be akin to admitting to the very thing that was making Olive's expression smug and what was most certainly the absolute last thing that Ava wanted, I bit my tongue. Saying those words aloud would probably also earn me a third bullet wound, one that would be courtesy of Ava and her prized possession, a rifle named Luna.

I'd been shot once in the last twenty-four hours.

That was enough.

When neither Ava nor I said anything, Olive closed the door and moved over to the wall of cabinets, peppering me with questions about how I was feeling while washing her hands in the sink. She shut off the faucet, pulled on some gloves, and tugged at the corner of the bandage.

"Looks good," she said, poking at the edges of the wound.

I was barely aware of the doctor's actions, my focus on Ava, her face going blank as she turned away from me, went to the computer, and bent to snag the flash drive from the computer.

Then she was gone.

The door shutting behind her with the barest sound.

And I was left with the feeling that I'd made both progress in getting behind those heavy walls of hers, and that I'd also helped supply her the rebar to strengthen them.

SIX

Ava

I PUSHED into the gym and stopped.

"Seriously?"

Dan glanced up at me with a guilty expression, quietly setting the weight he'd been lifting down. "What?"

It had been two days since the mission. One since he'd passed out unconscious.

And approximately seven minutes since Olive and Laila had left for KTS's main headquarters.

"*This* is rest?" I asked, nodding at the weight bench.

"It's light."

Since the thirty-five-pound dumbbells he'd been casually lifting were damn near my maximum, I simply lifted a brow and said, "Would Olive think these are light?"

A flash of temper on his face, one I saw so infrequently that it actually took me by surprise, his dark tone even more so. "I like and respect you, Ava," he muttered. "But you're neither my mother nor my doctor. I've played by Olive's rules for twenty-four hours and will continue to do so." He picked the weight back up and began curling it again. "I promised to do light duty for two weeks," he said. "I'm not back-flipping over here. I'm exercising—if sitting on my ass and lifting less than half my normal weight can be considered exercising."

His irritation should have been off-putting.

Instead, it made him more likeable.

I'd never seen him grumpy, and seeing him a little grouchy made him seem more human, especially after I'd elevated him onto such a tall pedestal for these last years. Maybe we weren't quite the leaps and bounds apart I'd always thought. Maybe we were just two people who—

And *that* was the crazy talking.

Dan, as an agent, was admirable. He was the kind of even, steady co-worker who I knew I could rely on. Ego didn't get in his way, and he wasn't afraid to lead if the situation required it, or to step back and let others take charge.

Dan, as a man, was similar. He was smart, funny, even-keeled. And while he was confident, he wasn't one of those guys who had to prove his dick was big—

Speaking of which . . . those sweatpants he was wearing, yo.

They were definitely pointing to the fact that he had nothing to prove on that front—it was a simple fact of nature.

He shifted and I tore my gaze away, fully aware this was dangerous territory.

Talk of pedestals and similarities and thinking we had anything more in common than our line of work was insane.

"I'm well-aware of my limits," he said.

"You're right," I agreed.

"And," he rattled off, picking up the weight and curling it

again, and I didn't think he'd actually heard me, had just expected me to disagree with him exercising, so was already prepared with his counterargument. "I also know that I can't expect to sit on my ass for a few weeks and come out of this strong."

"You're right," I repeated.

"And further that," he began.

I sat on the bench next to him, snagged the weight from his hand. "Dan," I said. "I just told you *you're right* twice in fifteen seconds. Take the victory and shut up."

"You—" He froze. "You just said *I* was right?"

"Yeah, yeah," I mock-grumbled, setting the weight on the floor. "Don't rub it in."

A smile curved his lips, and I inhaled, my hands curling into fists. The urge to reach out and touch him was strong, so strong that I actually found myself standing again, heading toward the door.

This was why I didn't spend time with him any longer, why I hardly spent time with *anyone*. Laila was the only exception, and my team leader had pretty much bullied me into friendship, or at least, she'd pestered me into it, dragging Olive into the mix for good measure. But those connections made me nervous. Shit got real when feelings were involved, and I'd been careful to not feel anything more than respect and professional admiration for anyone.

First Laila. Then Olive. Then Dan—

No.

"Hey."

His voice was close enough that I had to lock down my body in order to not react and not to react violently.

Calm. *Calm.*

The man was recovering from a gunshot wound.

I could *not* knock him on his ass.

"You okay?"

Slightly hysterical laughter bubbled up in my throat, and I swallowed hard to prevent it from escaping. "Just peachy," I said, reaching for the door handle.

Except for the fact that I was ridiculously attracted to this man I worked with, a man who was dangerous to me, who was insightful and would look too deeply into my past, who, once he knew all the dark fucking secrets of said past, would look at me in disgust.

That was the danger that laid down the path of me thinking I might be able to have a normal relationship with anyone, with him.

That couldn't be.

His hand dropped onto my shoulder, spun me gently to face him. "What is it, Ava?"

I took a page out of his book and said, "I'm fine."

"That's a lie," he said. "Something happened. And it's not me getting shot or Olive's orders. What put that look into your eyes?"

My past.

That's what put it into my eyes.

My past once again reminding me that I wouldn't ever be normal.

"Dan," I said, shaking my head, stepping out from beneath his hand. "I—"

And fucking horror of all horrors, my voice broke.

He came closer, reached out as though he were going to hug me. God, it was pathetic how much I wanted to be hugged by him, to be held gently against his chest. The last time the team had been in San Francisco, I'd watched him hug his sister, had envied the statuesque blond hockey player.

I hadn't ever been hugged.

Not by a parent. Not by a family member. Not by a friend

or lover. I'd not known what I was missing at first, and later, I hadn't been able to let anyone get that close.

But Dan had hugged me.

That week on the orchard he'd held me close, stroked his fingers through my hair.

And I'd liked it . . . too damned much.

"Don't," I said, skittering back when he came closer.

One sharp word.

"Hey," he said, his hand brushing my arm again, "you can—"

One sharp *movement*.

I spun out of his grip in one of those moves I'd practiced over and over and *over* again in my twenty-nine years, until it had become instinctive, until it had been permanently ingrained in my muscle memory.

"Oof," he grunted as I pinned him against the door, my elbow to his throat.

"Don't," I repeated, holding him for only a second before guilt swelled up and bubbled over. I was manhandling someone who'd been shot all of two days before. What kind of sick fuck did that?

A Toscalo did.

A member of my fucked-up family did.

Because violence was ingrained in my blood, my history, my DNA.

Because I was just as bad as the rest of them.

"Ava—"

I pushed past him, wincing again when he grunted in pain. But I didn't have the strength to stop, not when my eyes burned with tears, not when I was feeling so weak inside.

Not when I might reveal *everything*.

SEVEN

Dan

IT WASN'T until two weeks later that I saw Ava again.

After the incident at the gym, I'd stifled the urge to go after her, deciding she needed some space. But a few hours later, when I'd gone to the room she'd been assigned, I'd found it empty, any sign of her presence erased.

Well, except for the faint scent of peaches in the air.

But no clothing had been left behind, the bed had been stripped. All of the towels had been removed from the attached bathroom, the sink cleaned, the counters wiped down.

Ava was gone, having requested leave to coincide with the light duty I was on for two weeks.

She'd left me in Munich, split off from my team while they dealt with the information on the flash drive.

Not that they'd intentionally cut me out.

Ava had given me my own copy of the data, asked me to get my brain working on making heads or tails of it until I felt up to traveling to KTS's main headquarters and meeting up with them. So, I'd hung in Germany for a few days, recovering on Olive's orders, feeling mostly fine, if a bit weak still, but I hadn't returned to England right away because part of me had expected Ava to show up. For us to go through the files together.

Before the gym incident, we might have.

Before I'd pushed, she might have stayed, might have allowed me to inch closer.

But I'd pressed her.

And she'd gone.

Some agent, huh?

I'd been impatient and driven Ava away, and now I'd spent the last two weeks pouring over some fucking files on a flash drive that made up a puzzle I didn't have any clue how to solve.

Now, I itched to apologize, even knowing she would dismiss it, that she would pretend I had nothing to say sorry for.

And as stupid as it was, as clear as she'd made it to me she didn't want it, I still wanted to hug her.

To hold her close and erase whatever had made her so sad.

Which was laughable, I knew that.

Still, even with me knowing that, the urge to comfort didn't go away. I was a protector by nature. She was a teammate, and that alone would have been enough for me to put my life on the line for her. But she was also a person I respected, and just because she could hit a target from over a thousand meters and could kick my ass in hand-to-hand combat didn't mean that the urge to protect just disappeared.

Of course, all of that was complicated by the fact that she was a woman I wanted with a need that bordered on desperation.

I'd had a glimpse of that oasis in the desert, and I wanted more.

"Thanks for coming," the object of that desperation said to the small group that had gathered in the conference room.

Our whole team was there—Laila and her husband, Ryker, Olive, me, and Ava.

Five people with one goal. Five people who made up one of many teams at KTS, all with that same goal.

To protect the innocent.

In whatever format that required.

We all murmured our greetings then sat back and got ready to listen. Ava hooked up a laptop to a dongle, and the familiar files I'd been going through line-by-line over the last two weeks appeared on the monitor on the wall.

Lettuce.

Fucking lettuce shipments.

It made no sense. We all knew the data on the USB couldn't just simply be lettuce shipments, but neither our team, nor the specialized technical arm of KTS had been able to unearth any hidden data or deduce a code that indicated the seemingly innocuous shipments and invoices were more than produce.

We would keep working, of course, but none of us had made any headway to date.

Except, perhaps, Ava.

Because she had heavy dark circles under her eyes, and though her cheeks were pinkened as if she'd spent too much time in the sun, her skin beneath that reddened patch was pale.

She glanced at Laila, who nodded encouragingly.

"We all know this isn't about lettuce." She tapped a button on the keyboard, and lines appeared on the screen, circling and highlighting data. I watched as the program ran, rearranging columns and shifting rows, pooling the information within until . . . holy shit.

My mouth dropped open. Because was that really—?

"This isn't just about the Mikhailova clan," she said. "It's also about the Toscalo family."

EIGHT

KTS Headquarters
Northeast England
15:09hrs local time

Ava

I STARED AT THE SCREEN, watching the program I'd spent every minute of the last week writing work. From the moment I'd first seen the correlation, the possibility that this ring had involved my family had been churning around in my head.

It was why I'd been so rattled during the incident with Dan.

The possibility had occurred to me that morning, one that seemed all too likely based on the knowledge I carried from my childhood. And even though I'd wanted to pretend it wasn't the truth, wanted to avoid the reality that my family had dipped low even on their scale of despicable, the evidence was there.

They were working with the Mikhailova clan, and they were trading in people.

In. People.

Fucking disgusting.

And I'd grown up in their painful embrace.

I wanted to pretend to be unaffected and unbothered that the people who were responsible for my being on this planet were fucking evil.

Turned out, pretending didn't make a fucking bit of difference.

Two weeks ago in Germany, I'd deduced the first piece, the tendril of a memory coming to the surface as my eyes had fallen onto a line of data. I'd remembered a code shown to me in boastful pride to hide protection money my family collected from the businesses on *their* streets, and . . . it had fit.

I'd needed to move, to take a break, to avoid the truth.

I'd gone to the gym that morning and I'd stumbled upon the very man who could so easily deduce that truth, could see too deeply, could perceive what was lurking beneath my calm mask.

Now I was about to share part of that truth, part of the secret I'd hidden from everyone save Laila. But even she didn't know the full breadth of my depravity, couldn't begin to understand all the things I'd seen and done and blindly turned an eye to.

The memories of those deeds, those horrible events, those actions I would never be able to make right, meant I'd ended up in the gym with a need to run and sweat and work myself into oblivion. I'd been so off my game and too easily read and frankly . . . too fucking fragile. So after that conversation in the gym, I'd known I'd needed to go, had needed space to think without constantly feeling rubbed raw by Dan and his presence.

I should have been able to lock down my emotions.

From the moment I'd been old enough to finally understand my family was cruel and involved in absolutely abhorrent things, from the moment I'd stopped blindly abiding them, from trying to *be* like them—of course that had come far too late and was something I would never forgive myself—I'd worked to shut off all my feelings. It was the only way to survive as I'd worked to distance myself from them, from the things they did, and to buy me time to find an escape route.

They'd seen, though, understood they were part of something that had disgusted me, and they'd tried all methods of manipulation and gaslighting to bring me to their side.

And when it became clear I would *never* abide by what they were doing, they'd—

"Holy shit," Olive breathed, thankfully pulling me from my memories. "Is that their shipping pattern?"

I sucked in a silent breath, slowly released it, then nodded. "Yes," I said, highlighting the columns. "These are the shipments we've been able to confirm from the last six months"— most of which KTS had arrived too fucking late to help the men, women, and children from being trafficked—"and I believe these are their scheduled drops for the next three months." I pointed to a row. "This is an example of a planned pickup." I gestured to another. "This, I think, is for a merchandise drop-off."

Merchandise being people.

"Holy hell," Olive said. "Why are they all in Italy?"

"And they're definitely not for fucking lettuce," Dan muttered. "How did you—?"

His eyes, an azure that reminded me of the deep blue water of the Mediterranean. I'd grown up overlooking that sea, first walking on the sandy shores and later keeping hold of the barest sliver of my sanity by staring out the crack in the stone wall I'd managed to carve out.

My fingertips ached, remembering how I'd bloodied my nails, scratching against that wall, hour after hour.

I'd grown up in the arms of the Italian mob, had been honed in the blood and violence of turf wars and money laundering and drug smuggling.

It had taken me years to find my way out, years more to

find KTS.

But I'd been working with the agency for almost a decade, doing good things, finding a way to erase my blood-stained past. All it took was one source, one flash drive, one set of files, and I felt like I was dumped right back there.

In that cell.

In that darkness.

Just a sliver of the sea keeping me sane.

"They're working with the Mikhailova," I said. "It's why we haven't been able to shut the Russian ring down before. They're not running it out of Russia. They're running it out of Italy."

Ryker, Laila's husband and their most experienced agent, frowned. "Where are you getting your information?"

I couldn't deny I felt a slice of relief that Ryker didn't know my past. Laila was the only one who knew a little of how I'd grown up—or well, not the specific *how* when it came to cells and darkness and torture, but Laila knew that I had grown up in the fold of the mob. I had trusted her with that information before I'd allowed her to bring me to KTS, and she'd helped me build my cover as Ava Mills when I'd committed to the agency.

But my friend hadn't told Ryker.

Even though they were married.

And that made the brittleness that had filled my bones dissipate slightly. How much to tell the team would be *my* decision.

But there wasn't any doubt in this situation.

I would tell them everything I knew, anything that might be helpful. Because I'd left any loyalty to the Toscalos behind the moment I'd escaped that cell and gone to ground.

"My information is from someone directly linked to the Toscalo family," I murmured.

"Who?" Dan asked.

Even with the determination to share, my pulse picked up, my throat went tight. I'd hidden this truth because I didn't want anyone to think I was like them, to look at me differently because of my past.

But fuck if I was a coward.

I hadn't survived and gone on to fight for those who couldn't by pussying out when things got tough. Lifting my chin, sucking in a breath, I met Dan's gaze.

"Me."

Silence.

For a long time.

Then Olive spoke. "What do you mean *you?*"

"I mean," I said, having to force the words out because it had been so fucking long, and it was so fucking painful to think it, let alone to give voice to it. "I mean, I am Evelina Toscalo, daughter of Frankie Toscalo, and the woman who was supposed to have been the heir to the Toscalo family." I glanced at Ryker. "That's how I knew the code. Before I left, my cousin showed it to me. He'd put it together to hide income—though it took me a bit to remember how to make the puzzle pieces come together."

This time, there wasn't silence in response to my revelation.

This time, there was a flurry of noise.

From Ryker and Olive and Dan, all talking over each other, all throwing questions my way.

"Yo!" Laila called sharply.

I sucked in a breath, thankful for the interruption to the peppering of statements.

"Ava will explain," she said. "But you got to let the woman talk."

Ryker lifted a brow at his wife. "You knew."

Laila slanted a glance his way. "I know lots of things. I also know that when you ran your own team, you didn't always share every bit of information with your significant other."

Meaning her.

The slightly chastising tone shut Ryker up—because it was

true—and relaxed me enough that I could begin to answer some of the questions slung my way.

"Yes, my real name is Evelina Toscalo," I said to Ryker. "But I haven't been her for a long time. No," I directed at Olive, "Evelina isn't dead. Clearly. It was just safer for me to make everyone think that. And yes, I spent eighteen years in the mob," I told Dan. "Unfortunately, I wasn't good at faking I was on their side back then. Eventually, they came to recognize I wasn't ever going to be their good little heiress, and so they . . ." *No.* My eyes slid to the side, and I forced the memories of darkness and pain away. Only then did I meet Laila's gaze. "The reason I knew about this code at all, is because of Sergio. He's the real heir now, even though that information isn't commonly known. He bragged to me a few times about a shell game he'd created"— one that had effectively made him, and not my younger brother, my father's successor—"and when I saw the files, I remembered some of the code." I glanced down at my hands. "My computer and the algorithm I wrote did the rest."

After a moment of silence, I looked up, saw the wide eyes greeting me.

"All this being said, I can't be certain they're even still using the same code more than a decade later. Nor even that Sergio is still the heir," I admitted, sinking into my chair and leaning back into the plush leather. "The truth is, none of this may be right, and it could all be about fucking lettuce."

Olive snorted.

"I know," I said. "I know it's not about lettuce. I just . . . I don't want you all to think I magically cracked this when it may not be right any longer."

"Right," Laila said. "Well, there's only one way for us to know for sure."

My brows drew together. "How?"

"We're taking a trip to Italy and getting some lettuce."

NINE

Dan

WHITE SAND.

Crystal clear water.

Human trafficking.

One of those things didn't belong with the others.

Or the multitude of tourists crowding the beaches wouldn't think so, anyway. They were captivated by the natural beauty, the warm weather, the soothing waves. They also had absolutely no understanding of the dark underworld that shadowed the island.

Namely, that the tourism industry in this part of the country was ruled by the Toscalo family.

Visitors didn't understand the friendly male who delivered their drink beachside was a migrant, paid pennies on the dollar, and drawn into service because he was unable to get papers to work legally. They didn't know that the poverty seen just inland was because organized crime made it difficult to make a legitimate living.

They just saw the pretty beaches, the friendly locals, and opened up their wallets.

But I wasn't here to take down the entire Italian mob—though it would be a nice side project. Rather, the rest of the team and I were here to investigate Ava's assessments about the data, and if they proved right, we might be able to interrupt a shipment.

Of people.

Fuck, that made me sick.

It made me want to hunt the fuckers down who thought it was somehow okay to trade in people—in children and women and men who were vulnerable—and obliterate each and every one of them.

I might be able to take down a decent chunk of them before I went down, but the killing done by my hands wouldn't *do* anything.

Yes, it would make me feel better.

Yes, maybe some vengeance would be enacted.

But the crimes wouldn't stop, and neither would the exploitation, the trafficking, the illegal drugs.

So, instead of loading up with weapons and going on some *I will find you-Taken* movie vendetta, I sat in the fucking lounge chair and accepted the drink from the man who was a pawn of the Toscalo family with a "Thank you," a smile, and slipping a large enough tip into his hand that maybe someday, if he got enough of them, the man might be able to eventually get out.

Then I sat there and sipped the whiskey and waited.

For my "girlfriend."

Before Laila and Ryker had gotten hitched and Ryker was running his own team, I probably would have been paired with our team leader or stashed at the bar like Laila was, watching my back. But now that things between her and Ryker were legal and Ryker had gotten his possessive angry eyes down pat, I knew it was better for my physical well-being to not be playing Laila's doting boyfriend.

Plus, Laila didn't speak fluent Italian. Not like—

"Hi, baby."

I stilled, trying not to let my jaw drop open and failing miserably.

Because . . .

Ava.

She had peeled off after we'd arrived at the hotel to "freshen up and change into my swimsuit"—though that hadn't been all she was doing. She'd also been setting cameras and placing microphones that Olive, Laila, and Ryker would monitor.

Because if Ava was right, the exchange would be happening somewhere on this hotel's property in one day's time.

In a crowded, tourist-filled building, during one of the busiest weekends in the summer.

The Toscalo family had balls, that was for damn sure.

Kind of like the woman standing in front of me wearing a positively tiny string bikini. Breasts. Hips. Thighs. Miles of creamy skin. A large hat shaded her face, and fuck, she was a wet dream come to life. I nearly begged her to spin around so I could see that luscious ass.

I didn't.

Because Luna was probably around somewhere, and I didn't feel like getting shot again.

Ava lifted a brow, and a moment too late I scrambled up, remembering to play the role of boyfriend. "Baby?" I asked softly, leaning in to kiss her cheek and gesturing for her to take the lounge chair.

"Would you prefer Boner?" she returned chipperly.

I ignored the name and countered, "Where's your weapon?" I knew she wouldn't be without one.

One brown brow came up as she lowered herself onto the chair. "Where do you *think* it is?"

I grinned, tore my gaze from her body, and sat down on the sand next to her. "Are we only going to talk to each other in questions from now on?"

Scanning the horizon, she asked, "How do *you* feel about questions?"

I snorted.

"Knife in my purse," she said, breaking the question streak. "Plastic pistol hidden in the flowers of the hat. Stiletto in the frame of my glasses. You?"

"Blades in both flip-flops. Handgun in my backpack."

"Good." She shifted in the chair. "Everything in my quadrant is in place. Bags made it safely to our room. Laila and Ryker are next door. As planned, Olive is on the floor below, so we have access to the stairwell."

"Have you seen any of your family?"

That was part of the reason she'd been the one to place the cameras. She could move like the wind, melt into shadows, *and* she knew who to look out for.

"Yes," she said. "Three cousins. What about you?"

I nodded at a cabana tucked beneath several palm trees. It was draped in a white gauzy material, but even from fifty feet away, we could see the group of men inside. "No Toscalos. But some of the Mikhailova clan are inside. Three *bratok*"—soliders—"meeting with their brigadier. I didn't get a clear look at his face, but it appears to be Alexander Ivankov. The *bratok* are definitely his, and familiar faces—Konstantin, Boris, and Sergei."

"Dumb, Dumber, and Dumbest," she muttered.

"Yeah, too bad Ivankov isn't any of those."

"No, unfortunately he is too fucking smart for his own good." Swarmy and somehow always able to squirm out of any charges we managed to pin on him.

"But at least he has a dumb name," I said lightly.

Her gaze slanted to mine. "True, Iceberg isn't great," she said referring to the alphabet-based portion of the code we were working based on the information that she'd presented earlier. The correlation between the known associates in both groups and their alphabetic name had been the simplest part, once they knew what to look for. "But it isn't Boner," she teased.

"Shut it, Mud."

The man who'd brought me the drink earlier, came up before she could reply and took Ava's order.

I didn't speak Italian, but I knew enough to recognize the order.

It made me smile.

"A peach daiquiri?"

She turned to me, her eyes narrowed, even as flashes of memories from two years ago flared bright in my mind. The tart-sweet of peach juice on her lips, her tongue.

"You got a problem with that?"

"No." I leaned closer, near enough to smell the coconut of her sunscreen, the soft floral scent of her shampoo. "It's just a little . . ."

"If you finish that sentence with girly, I'll reacquaint you with Luna."

"I love Luna," I said as the man returned with the slushie peach drink and handed it to her. I noticed that she slipped the server a folded-up bill, exactly as I had earlier.

She took a sip and sighed in pleasure.

Which made my cock twitch. Cute. So glad my teenage boy could make an appearance while on a mission with a woman I wanted almost more than my next breath.

"Sure, you do," Ava said. "So long as you aren't looking down her barrel."

I snorted. "That's true."

She pulled out her cell, pretended to be texting, but I could see she was taking several pictures of the trio. "What if this isn't what we think?"

"You're right with the code, Ava." I leaned against the lounge chair, dug my bare feet into the warm sand. "You're the best agent I know. Hands down. And even if there's more to this, or it's not exactly what it seems, all we have to do is look at that cabana and have confirmation that serious shit has gone down."

"Yeah," she whispered. "And if he *is* Iceberg, he showed up a lot in the files."

I nodded. "Along with Romaine, who you've pegged as Romeo," I said, sympathy spreading through me. I wasn't surprised she'd survived growing up in a lion's den. Ava was the strongest woman I knew, and considering I was surrounded by strong women on a daily basis, that was no joke. "Your younger brother. Are you—"

"He's not my brother."

A sharp rebuttal that should have brought a chill to the hot Mediterranean climate, it was filled with so much frost, but though I met her eyes, I didn't say anything to deny it, didn't argue with her about DNA and family. I was close to my sister, considered her one of my best friends when I was Stateside and could actually see her, but I knew I was one of the lucky ones. Genes, unfortunately, didn't create love, nor loyalty, nor kindness.

And I didn't need to be able to understand the finer points of DNA nor every bit of what happened to Ava growing up, to understand that family often carried complications right alongside it.

The shadows were right there in her eyes.

An innocent girl growing up in the mob.

Fuck, how had she survived?

Except . . . I *knew* how she survived. It was clear as day in the same intensity and spirit that had brought me to the training mat often enough, the same focus that had made her the best shot in the agency, even with her needing to wear glasses.

Speaking of which, if we were sitting on our asses, just watching our targets laugh and drink, I might as well change the subject to something that wouldn't weigh so heavily on her.

"Why didn't you ever do Lasik?"

Brown eyes, surrounded by thin black frames, came to mine. "I wasn't a candidate for it," she said. "My eyesight isn't all that bad. I'm fine up close, but at a distance, one eye struggles. My right optic nerve was damaged."

"I'm guessing it wasn't damaged during an op."

"No." A beat. "And it turns out, I wasn't receptive to the lesson my father wanted to teach me."

I read between the lines and felt like the biggest asshole on the planet because I hadn't changed the subject at all. Instead, I'd ended up drawing her focus right back to her blood relatives, right into the childhood she'd given the briefest overview of back at headquarters. I'd read between the lines the week before, too, understanding that during the briefing, there was a lot more she *hadn't* said than she had.

So, me bringing her attention back to her family was right up there with Mud smooth.

Brit mentally smacked me across the head, but I didn't need it. I already knew that the surefire way to get through those walls, to get Ava to trust me, was to *not* continue to poke at the open wound that was her family.

Shit.

"Tell me about the cameras," I said, settling on something

safer, even as the still-healing injury on my chest and back ached, reminding me of all the poking Olive had done nearly three weeks ago. I wouldn't say she was strictly happy that I'd moved from light duty straight into a mission, but the team had needed to move quickly, and we'd made sure to have two other KTS teams on standby nearby, in case Ava's theory panned out.

"I took care of the corridors and stairwells," she said. "Olive is going to take care of several of the service areas. I don't think any of us are expecting them to transport lettuce here on the beach, but we'll make sure those are covered once it's full dark."

"Agreed."

We would keep eyes on the situation, step in and interrupt any "lettuce" shipment if it came to fruition, making sure to do so with only enough firepower to make sure no innocents were harmed.

Our charge for this particular mission was to gather intel and to document any evidence of the Toscalo family and the Mikhailova clan working together. That included—

"Damn," she whispered. "They really are part of this, aren't they?"

I turned carefully to look where she indicated with a bob of her head, glancing to the right, to the man I recognized from KTS's files on the Toscalo family. Since we were less familiar with the Italian mob, we'd spent our time on the flight over going through them. Which meant I knew from a glance that the man was Romeo Toscalo, Ava's younger brother. Romeo strode through the sand, heading straight for the cabana where he shook hands with Ivankov, the two men laughing like they were old friends meeting for a fun afternoon, rather than two fucking bastards of humanity who were suspected of being involved in a variety of criminal activities around the globe.

Activities, until Ava's algorithm, KTS had never connected.

We had always treated the crime families of Italy and the

Russian mafia both as adversaries who needed to be taken down, but we never received intel that those adversaries may be working together.

"Romeo and Ivankov," Ava muttered, sitting up and shifting closer when I pulled out my cell. We faked doing a selfie, while actually capturing several high-resolution shots of the meeting, and though this was work—just simple reconnaissance—the way Ava felt curled against my back as we faked our way through a few photographs definitely had nothing to do with KTS or criminal masterminds.

It was me and Ava.

That thread connecting us.

Normally, Ava was all sharp words and extreme focus—or she'd been that way before our time together and after. But during that week, she'd relaxed. She'd given me a glimpse of the woman inside, and I'd fallen fucking hard.

I'd thought it was the start of something.

In the end, she'd made it clear it was nothing more than sex and a good time and that she was going to move to another team if I continued pursuing her.

What could I do?

I either let her go, cherished the memories, and contented myself with the small slice of her in my life as it was, or I pushed . . . and lost all of her.

So, even though I missed the closeness we'd developed that week—talking old missions and TV shows and movies, eating and drinking, and yes, making love to the woman I adored—I knew when she slammed that door that I had to step back.

But I still grieved for what I'd lost. That feeling of utter rightness wasn't something I'd ever found with anyone else, and the way my soul just settled when I was with her . . .

It made it really hard to let her go.

Because she was sharp words and quiet confidence on the

outside, but so damned special inside, and that need to delve deeper, to see more, made it increasingly more difficult to ignore the draw I felt toward her.

But . . . she didn't want that.

A strand of her hair brushed my shoulder and before I realized what I was doing, I'd shifted, turning so I could face her.

At the contact, we both froze, nearly nose-to-nose, close enough that I could smell the fruity aroma of her shampoo, the peach scent of her drink on her tongue, our breaths intermingling. And she didn't shift back, didn't retreat, just stared at me with unfathomable eyes.

My lips tingled. Heat that had nothing to do with the climate and everything to do with the beautiful person in front of me slid over my skin. It would be so easy to just close the distance between us, to lean the slightest bit closer and taste—

Work.

Fucking focus, man.

This wasn't a woman I was trying to seduce for a quick fuck.

This was Ava.

This was a woman I wanted forever, even if the long game took two more years.

And we were on a potentially dangerous mission, one that had to have her feeling rubbed raw on the inside because it involved her family—even though her family had to be more of a bad memory than any real connection to her flesh and blood in the present.

We spent the next thirty minutes outwardly enjoying our drinks on the beach, even as we kept our attention on the meeting in the tent.

The two men were attended by a variety of scantily clad women, bringing bottles to the cabana by the bucketful. Loud laughter drifted across the beach, even as Ivankov's three goons sat stonily behind their leader.

Romeo, meanwhile, was completely at ease as he continued to refill his glass.

Neither man seemed apt to move.

"We've got the images," I said. "Let's go back to the room and regroup. If this is going down tonight or tomorrow, we need to be prepared."

Still not thinking, or rather, thinking too deeply of all the things I wanted but didn't think I'd ever get to have, I extended my hand, half-surprised and yet not surprised at all when she took it and stood. Perhaps, she'd kept that deliberate distance between us, but Ava was also a KTS agent, and we were on that potentially dangerous mission. She would never do anything to compromise that, even if it meant pretending to be a doting girlfriend.

I snagged my flip-flops and she pulled away to slip into a cover-up, tugging it from the bag I hadn't bothered to give a second look to because I'd been drooling over that sexy as hell bikini.

A strand of her hair slipped in front of her face, and I stepped toward her, tucking it behind her ear before I'd even realized I'd moved.

"What was that?" she asked.

Insanity, I thought. Pushing when I shouldn't. Giving in to temptation when I'd promised myself I would be patient and give her space, take time to win her trust.

But what I said aloud was, "Just making sure you have a clear line of sight."

Which didn't make any sense.

Like *no* sense.

But it was the first thing that had come out of my mouth, and I had no choice but to go with it.

Her brows drew down. "Dan—"

"You can't see if it's in your face."

Sparks in pale brown eyes. "Are you fucking serious?"

My earpiece buzzed, and, saved by the bell, I surreptitiously touched the spot behind my ear, seeing Ava do the same out of the corner of my eye.

"Room. Five minutes," came Laila's voice.

Since neither of us were wearing mics, we couldn't answer, but without another word, we both made our way across the beach and into the hotel.

Well, there were five more words.

"Don't make me get Luna." Ava glared up at me, and I knew the long game was still really fucking long, but instead of answering, I just held the door so she could enter the lobby.

I did smile though.

Because threats were so much better than being iced out.

So, maybe the long game wasn't quite as long as I'd thought.

The lobby was filled with people checking in and out, making their way to the multitude of restaurant offerings. Carts full of Louis Vuitton luggage were pushed speedily through the crowd, many a pair of expensive high heels clicking across the marble floor. We skirted the throng, threaded the needle of lush plants dotting the walls, and made it onto the blessedly empty elevator.

I breathed a sigh of relief, hating the crowd, hating how it made Ava vulnerable, made it nearly impossible to assess every threat.

The doors began to slide closed, gleaming bronze metal reflecting the beach-ready forms.

Ava turned her head toward me, lips parting—

A hand kept the doors from closing, gripping the metal panel then pushed them open.

Unease prickled down my spine as three suited men stepped onto the elevator.

We were trapped.

TEN

Ava

HORROR FILLED ME FOR A LONG, interminable moment, freezing me in place.

But just as quickly as that horror came on—horror at seeing my uncle through the open elevator doors, trailed by two of my cousins—I remembered myself, remembered my training, remembered the instincts honed by hour after hour of hard work.

I spun toward Dan, stepped into his arms, and slanted my mouth across his.

He didn't move for long enough that I felt a bubble of panic well within me, tightening the back of my throat, sending my pulse skittering.

Then he wrapped his arms around me, pinned me to the elevator wall, and kissed me back.

Oh, *how* he kissed me back.

I was only distantly aware of my surroundings, *far* more distantly than I should have been, based on the fact that the person who'd caused the injury to my eye was currently chuckling and stepping onto the elevator.

But I was having difficulty focusing on anything except for the feel of Dan's hands on my body, his lips against mine, soft yet demanding, his tongue slipping into my mouth, tangling with mine. There shouldn't be any tongue in this fake kiss. There shouldn't be this much contact, or heat, or—

A throat cleared, and we froze.

"What floor?" my uncle, Fabio, said in Italian.

And fuck, I hated that his voice sent a sliver of fear down my spine.

Dan slowly pulled his lips from mine, breathing elevated and puffing against my mouth. Our eyes locked for a heartbeat before he pressed my face lightly into his chest. "Pardon?" he asked, playing up the notes of Southern in his voice.

"Ah," Fabio replied, switching to English. "American. What floor?"

"Eight," Dan said, lying about the floor we were actually on. I was on the same page, knew we'd go up to eight and double back using the stairs, just to be safe so Fabio wouldn't know where our room was. The lie was the same reason he'd run his fingers through my hair, shifting my hat slightly so it covered my face more fully.

I didn't *think* my family would recognize me. My face had matured, my hair had darkened slightly, and I had my glasses on. But it wasn't like I'd had major plastic surgery. My facial structure was still my facial structure, and I couldn't deny I had many of the features of the Toscalo genetics.

Maybe Fabio wouldn't identify me from across a room or through a crowded hotel lobby, but I couldn't guarantee he wouldn't recognize me from three feet away.

"Honeymoon?" Fabio asked.

"First vacation together." Dan's fingers didn't stop stroking my hair.

I wasn't a woman who needed comfort, but I would be hard-pressed to deny that the gentle touch soothed the ball of panic deep in my gut. I loved the way I felt when he touched me. It had become an addiction during that week two years ago, one I'd barely been able to find the will to quit.

Cold turkey had been brutal.

But necessary.

Now he was touching me again, and—

Fabio laughed. "Ah, to have young love."

Dan chuckled. "I'm just lucky to have her at all."

"A romantic at heart. That will serve you well."

The doors dinged open, and I peeked out of the corner of my eye, watched as Fabio and my cousins exited the elevator.

My brother. My uncle. My cousins.

They were all here, infesting this beautiful hotel like the parasites they were.

The doors closed, leaving us in the empty metal box.

Neither of us moved.

"You okay?" Dan asked as the elevator began moving again.

Honestly?

I'd been on edge since the moment I'd seen Dan go down in the warehouse a few weeks ago. Frazzled when he'd passed out in my arms. As though my walls were crumbling to dust from the moment he'd come close in the gym. Raw from being back here, from seeing my family.

And melted from the inside out after that kiss.

Forgetting that rawness for a moment and not giving two shits that I'd been trapped in an elevator with a man who'd hurt me in the past.

Because the one who'd held and kissed me wouldn't.

Because *I* could protect myself.

That was what I needed to remember. The kisses and good feelings were just distractions. I needed to focus on the mission, on the job, on not *ever* being vulnerable again.

"I'm fine," I said and pushed against his chest. For a moment, it didn't seem like he would let me go. Then the elevator doors dinged, and he dropped his arms.

I ignored the slight blip of emptiness that came from stepping away from him, from losing the warmth of his body.

That kiss had been—

The doors started to close, and I slammed out a hand, holding them open.

Enough.

We were on a job, and I was daydreaming about a pair of lips.

I needed to get my shit together.

Otherwise, there was a strong possibility we were going to end up dead.

20:59HRS *local time*

I HAD my big girl clothes on.

Which was to say I had significantly more skin covered.

After we'd returned to one of the team's rooms, I'd manned the cameras and microphones for a bit while Ryker and Laila had played beach couple and Olive had provided backup. But the hours hadn't brought any further clarity, not that any of the team had necessarily expected them to. Not during the day, anyway. If something was going to happen, as we all very much suspected it would, it wouldn't be on the crowded beach or in the well-lit lobby. It would be at night.

In the service corridors or the underbelly of the hotel.

In the dark corners.

The parking lot.

The stairwells.

Which was why we had eyes on all of those, as well as the hallways and public areas. We'd drawn the line at putting cameras in rooms because we wanted to save the world, not spy on innocent people going about their days.

Of course, it would have been easier if we didn't have things like a moral compass. We could put cameras in every room, spy on each and every conversation.

Figure out exactly how deeply the two criminal families were intertwined.

All we would need to do is flip on a camera and hit record.

As it was, we'd already gone the slightly illegal route—but technically, *was* it illegal? We weren't bound by the typical regulations and standards most agencies had to abide by. Regardless of legality, we'd hacked into the hotel's registration system and isolated the suites that the Toscalo and Mikhailova groups were staying in. Which meant we now had access to the security feeds surrounding the rooms in addition to those from the cameras we'd planted.

The bad guys were covered.

Now, we just had to wait.

The trouble with waiting, however, was that it gave a woman too much time to think.

And unfortunately, what I was thinking at that moment was the fact that Dan was on the other side of a door and naked. He was showering, so it wasn't exactly like he was parading around, but I had a really good memory.

I'd touched that skin. Kissed every inch. Remembered *everything* in crystal clear detail.

Just to prove how sick my brain was, it had cataloged every inch of him. From the scar below his ribs to the shadowed squares that ridged his abdomen to the sharp Vs on his pelvis that disappeared into the waistband of his pants.

I'd carefully itemized it all.

And sometimes, late at night, when it was quiet and the weight of my childhood didn't seem so heavy, I wondered what it might be like.

To be with Dan.

The shower turned off, and I jumped, forcing my focus back to the monitors, but I found that the mirror was inconveniently —or conveniently, depending on one's point of view—positioned to showcase the door. Which was opening.

Which . . . showed Dan in nothing more than a towel.

Steam billowed out behind him like he was the hero of some Hollywood movie.

"Sorry," he murmured. "Forgot my bag."

A message appeared on my computer screen, Laila relieving me from my watch and telling me to get some rest, but to keep my phone on and be ready to go if the shipment happened.

We weren't sure how the spreadsheet counted time—the shipment was technically scheduled for tomorrow, but was that *midnight* tomorrow? As in three hours' time? Or late tomorrow evening, almost twenty-four hours from now? Since we weren't one hundred percent certain, we would cover all the bases.

"What did Laila say?" Dan asked.

I'd felt him come up behind me where I sat, but nothing could prepare me for the heat of his body, intensified by the shower, bringing a damp cloud of moisture with him that coated my skin and made me shiver.

"We're off watch for a few hours," I said, glancing back at

him. "Ryker's old team has it covered, but we're to be ready to go as needed."

He nodded then pointed at a square on the screen. "This camera might present a problem."

"Blind corner," I agreed. "Olive is already getting another camera in place."

"Good."

"Yeah."

He didn't move and neither did I. Dan, for his part, seemed riveted to the screen, but I was frozen in place by temptation.

If I moved, I might touch.

If I touched . . .

He straightened, and not a moment too soon. My fingers had clenched on my lap, resisting the urge to stroke that warm skin, but remaining there only by pure dint. Because that kiss. Because his smell. Because his body and the way he'd stroked my hair and how he'd held me so carefully.

And whiskey on his breath and on my tongue, mixing with peaches and rum.

Summer heat and sea breeze.

Gentle eyes in a gym.

Muddy hair and light bone.

Tempting. The man was far too tempting for a woman who didn't have any hope in hell of giving him what he deserved.

I turned my head and found my lips a mere inch from his, blazing blue eyes staring into mine, pinning me in place.

Just one inch, and I could taste him again.

Just one inch, and—

"I'll be right back," he said, stepping back.

"Dan—"

He stopped, straightening, that glorious chest on display. "Yeah?" he asked, a husky question that sent fire through my veins.

I opened my mouth but found the words were stoppered up in my throat.

"I—um . . ."

I wanted him. Just as I wanted so badly to pretend my past didn't exist, to have a moment with him, to maybe have more than *just* moments.

But that couldn't be.

We couldn't be.

"I moved your bag," I whispered, heart heavy even as I shored up the walls. Hoping and wanting didn't make one bit of difference. The only thing that mattered was reality. "It's by your bed."

He held my gaze for a heartbeat, lips parting, but then I looked away, pretending to turn back to the cameras, but in reality, watching him in the mirror as he scooped up his duffle bag and headed back into the bathroom.

"I'll be out in a minute."

I nodded but couldn't form words.

Not when every nerve in my body was telling me to trail after him into the bathroom, to dislodge that towel, perched so precariously around his hips. My words were bottlenecked by the need coursing through me, nearly propelling me to my feet and into that steam-filled room.

It would be so easy.

It would be so *good*.

That kiss had been the ultimate tease, bringing me back to two years ago. How good it had felt to give in to the fiery attraction, the sparking desire, the connection between us. I'd forgotten about my uncle, the elevator, the public place, and been right back in the humid summer days, eating peaches until my stomach hurt.

For a moment, I'd even forgotten about covering my back, about covering Dan's. I'd forgotten *everything*.

Because it felt so fucking good.

But . . . my feelings didn't matter.

The door clicked closed, and I stood, walking over to the windows. The curtains were drawn, but I knew if I shifted just slightly to the side, I could see a sliver of the sea, a glimmer of the beach below, and the sun sitting just below the horizon in the distance.

Maybe I should have felt trapped, the dim light of the room suffocating me, only the narrow slice of the outside world in front of me.

But I didn't feel contained.

This life I lived might, in many ways, be smaller than what most people hoped for, but it was more than I had ever dreamed up when locked in that cell.

I was strong and could protect myself. I'd spent the last years helping other people, undoing some of the bad in the world. I knew I could never hope to make up for what my family had done and what it currently still did, knew I couldn't begin to right every wrong.

But I had made some small difference.

Right now that was enough.

As was the truth I knew in the very marrow of my bones—I would never be back in that cell again.

Feeling slightly more centered, I turned away from the window.

Or started to, anyway.

Because just as I began to step back from the glass, I saw movement.

Coming in from the water.

And in the distance?

Boats.

A whole line of boats.

ELEVEN

Southern Italy
20:12hrs local time

Dan

THE KNOCK on the bathroom door sent my blood pumping, and for one instant, I thought that Ava had acted on the heat I'd seen in her eyes.

The same heat I was feeling.

Desire drawn tight after the kiss.

Since that day in the gym, I'd promised myself I wouldn't push her again, that I'd be patient until she made the next move. I'd soak up every nugget of information, file away every detail.

But I'd be patient and wait.

I just . . . hadn't known it would be so difficult.

She was so fucking strong and locked down, and yet I could feel her pain beneath those walls. And God, I just wanted to make it go away.

That was just wasn't reality.

I couldn't wish away pain and bad memories. I couldn't give her a decent family and an easy childhood. I—

The knock came again, sharper this time.

"Boots on," Ava said. "Two minutes ago."

Yanking myself out of my head, I didn't waste time by asking questions. I just yanked on my shirt, old habits making it so that I'd already put on my jeans, socks, and boots. I'd take a bare chest over bare feet any day of the week.

Turning the handle, I yanked open the door and stepped out into the hall. Ava thrust a bulletproof vest and jacket at my chest. "The beach."

I nodded, got busy strapping everything on, then reached for my gun. "Tell me."

Ava was checking Luna in rapid, efficient movements before breaking her down and putting her into a large beach tote. Inconvenient, yeah, but it wasn't like we could start running through the hotel with weapons.

"Boats about a hundred meters out. Olive and Ryker have already moved into position. They spotted Sergio and Romeo moving toward the dock behind the hotel." She lifted the bag onto her shoulder, busied herself strapping a blade to her thigh over her jeans, shoved her feet into her boots. "Laila is watching their backs at the bar while organizing the other teams."

I quickly checked my weapons, slid them into the various holsters. Guns on my chest, knives in my boots. "Where does she want us?"

"Rendezvous point six."

So, on the far side of the beach, behind the dock. "Got it." I shrugged into my jacket, headed for the door, and checked the peephole.

Clear.

I flicked open the bolt, tugged open the heavy wooden

panel, holding it wide and glancing back at Ava. "So, you and Luna ready for a midnight stroll?"

I'd checked the peephole.

But the peephole didn't show everything.

And by the time I processed that there was panic on Ava's eyes, by the time I'd recognized her reaching for her weapon, it was too late.

I spun, deflected one blow, dodged another.

Click.

"Put the gun down, Evelina."

I glanced over at Ava, saw the indecision on her face.

"Take the shot," I mouthed.

I knew she wouldn't miss. It was a fact of life, just as I knew the Earth revolved around the sun, that gravity pulled objects down, that I would give her my heart, if she only asked.

The barrel of a gun pressed against my temple. Hard.

"I can't," she mouthed, still holding her gun, but her eyes were flicking back and forth.

Fuck.

I knew then it wasn't that she didn't want to take the shot, but rather it was that she *didn't have the shot.*

I dropped my weight, got out of the first hold using one of the tricks I'd learned from her, spinning and kicking out, thrusting up with my elbow to knock the man who held me unconscious. Then I lurched back, intending to make it to the door, wanting it between me and Ava and the bad guys. We'd be trapped, but we would have more weapons and time to call in backup.

But there wasn't space to be had, wasn't space to move and maneuver.

Not when the hallway was crowded with fuckers speaking Italian and our backup wasn't in the room next door. Not when we were alone, and I couldn't make my way to Ava.

I saw movement out of the corner of my eye and ducked.

Not fast enough.

Something hard collided with my temple, exploded into red-hot pain.

And the last thing I heard before blackness swarmed up and pulled me under was Ava crying out my name.

UNKNOWN HRS *local time*

I DIDN'T KNOW how many hours had passed by the time I woke up.

But I emerged from unconsciousness, carefully slitting my eyes open and finding myself in pitch-black darkness with a foggy brain and a throbbing skull.

Carefully, I flexed my fingers, slowly getting the feeling back, then worked on my toes.

"You okay?" Ava whispered.

I froze, mid-toe flex. "I'm fine. You?"

"Dan," she warned, her voice shaking slightly. "Where are you injured?"

The shake did me in, made my heart squeeze tight, made me immediately want to repeat I was fine. But empty sentiments wouldn't reassure her, so I forced himself to focus, to take a breath, to cautiously move my arms and legs then sit up. "Nowhere," I said. "Besides a splitting headache, I'm good."

"Don't shit me."

"Where are you?" I asked.

"About five feet to your left," she said. "Careful, the ceiling is low."

Reaching overhead, I felt the roof of wherever the fuck we

were, and found it was indeed low, and covered with or hewn out of rough stone. I made my way over to her slowly, feeling for any openings or weak points.

There were none.

And before I knew it, I'd gotten to Ava.

I found her by bumping into her, and her hiss of pain sliced through me. "Ava, I'm not the one injured. Where are you hurt?"

"Knife wound in my abdomen. Didn't hit anything major, just I've lost a bit of blood." Her voice was quiet. Serious. "Patched it with the kit," she said, referring to the emergency supplies we all had stored in the tongue of our boots. "And the bleeding is under control. I took a bullet to my arm, only a glancing shot, so nothing to worry about there."

"But?" I asked, hearing the unspoken word.

"But," she said, "my ankle is broken."

Fuck. "How?"

"I went down wrong, caught my boot on the carpet."

I found her fingers in the dark. "How bad is the break?"

"Not good."

Shit.

"We'll figure it out." A squeeze. "Any idea where we are?"

"My uncle's special cell."

My heart seized. Her tone was dry and falsely calm because I could sense the note of terror beneath the surface. "Ava."

"Fate's laughing at me," she muttered. "I promised myself less than twenty-four hours ago that I would never be back here." She groaned. "And I'm only telling you this because if I freeze up, I might need you to kick my ass."

My lungs seized, but my tone was deliberately even. "Why would you freeze up?"

"Because this was where they would put me when I refused to do what they wanted, where I would sit in the dark and try my best to count the hours and sometimes the days before I heard another person's voice." She sighed. "I shouldn't be telling you any of this," she said. "It's the past, shouldn't have any bearing on the now."

"Except it does." She sucked in a breath. "So, what did they want you to do?"

Silence.

A long, quiet silence. "I can't talk about it. Not now. Maybe not ever."

"It's okay," I said, touching the back of her hand. "You don't have to talk about anything you don't want to."

She shifted slightly, and I wished I could see her face, but it was dark, too dark to make out anything more than the barest outline of her body.

"I wasn't like them," she whispered.

"I know."

"How?" she asked. "How could you possibly know?"

"Because I've spent these last years on this team with you, Ava. I know how well you shoot and that your rifle's name is Luna. I know you prefer the aisle seat on a plane. I know you don't have a sweet tooth, but you'll never turn down a bag of Fritos." I squeezed her fingers. "I've seen how you are with the kids we come across. They always turn to you. Because you're good inside."

She laughed, and it was a broken sound. "I'm not good inside. I'm broken and ruined and I've done things . . ." She cut herself off. "I've hurt people and killed. I'm not *good*."

"We've all killed," I said. "We've *all* done bad things."

"Dan." She sighed. "I've done more than bad things. I—"

"You fought them." I sucked in a breath and risked touching her cheek. "You wouldn't have ended up in this cell if you hadn't fought them."

A beat. "That doesn't make the rest of it okay."

"No," I said, filing that information away to process later, knowing that I wouldn't change her mind in this moment, and understanding that sometimes it didn't matter what anyone said.

The guilt never went away.

"How did you recognize where we are?"

"I was awake when they brought us down."

"Any idea of an exit route?"

"I have it mapped in my head."

"Good." I shifted so that I was lying next to her, wanting to keep her calm. Her voice was frosty, but it wasn't her usual chill. Rather it was an alpine river, just frozen over for the winter, its tumultuous current still flowing rapidly, right beneath the surface. Steady on top, panic below. "And this cell?"

A beat and I actually felt the tension leave her body when I gave her the out to stop focusing on the past and to think about the mission—or at least, to pool our resources on sorting out how to get the fuck out of this cell.

"At the dead end of a corridor. Heavy metal door. Hinges on the outside. No other exit."

"Well," I said on a sigh. "I've certainly had better accommodations."

She snorted.

"Where exactly is this special cell located?"

"Two clicks south of the hotel. Just above sea level at my father's mansion." She sighed. "But I'm not sure if the trackers"—all active agents had recently been implanted with GPS locating chips that could be activated by headquarters if shit got real—"will work beneath all this stone."

"So, we can either sit tight and see if they *do* work. Or—"

"Or we can do our best to get the fuck out of this shithole."

"I vote for option two," I said.

"Me, too." She pushed her elbows beneath her, and I helped her to gingerly sit up. "Okay." A short, pained sigh. "Here's what I know. The door is a metal plate, three feet in front of me. The exterior wall is made of stacked stone. There's a loose piece back behind where you were lying. If you tug it out, we'll be able to get a line of sight, and we might be able to put one of the trackers outside to ensure a signal."

That seemed like a reasonable place to start.

"Have you bound your ankle?"

"It's still in the boot." A beat. "I think it's better if it stays in for the time being."

I didn't like the sound of that, didn't like what that meant for her mobility, nor for how bad the actual injury was. "Where's the rock?"

"Lower left side of the far wall, about six inches from the floor. There's a piece that sticks out a bit. You should be able to get your fingers behind it."

I nodded. "Got it."

"Watch your head."

"Brit always says it's extra hard," I said, trying for light. "I'd be more likely to damage the rocks than my skull."

Ava snorted. "You do put the stub in stubborn."

I groaned. "That was a Ryker level joke."

She got quiet then said softly. "They're okay."

Except it was more question than statement and . . . it was something I hoped as well. Because if the Toscalos had found our room, they most likely had eyes on KTS and knew where all the agents were. And seriously, what a goddamned mindfuck—thinking we were the ones who had all the eyes, going in over-confident and thinking we were in control.

Then in the end, we'd been the ones ambushed.

Fuck.

"They had backup from the other KTS teams," I said, as much to convince myself as her. "I think they'll be in a better position than we are."

"You're right."

"Always."

She laughed lightly. "Nice try. Okay. Get your ass to that wall."

"Try not to stare at me as I move," I said, feeling in front of me as I crawled my way to the wall. "I know my ass is my best *ass*et."

"That is the worst joke I've ever heard."

"Even worse than Ryker's?"

"Fuck yes."

But my bad jokes and the lighthearted banter were distracting her, were subduing that buried panic in her tone, perking up her voice so she didn't seem so distraught and unlike herself.

The dry, calm Ava was back.

"How about you get your *ass* in gear?" she told me.

"Laila would be gagging about that one," I said, finding the little divot and trying to get my fat ass fingers behind it.

"She likes his bad jokes," Ava said. "Otherwise he wouldn't have married her."

"I suppose," I said.

"Did you find it?"

"Yeah," I said, tugging at the rock. "It's tight."

A beat.

Then, "That's what she said."

Freezing, not processing the statement at first, I nearly cracked my head on the low ceiling. Then I began to laugh. "Really?" I asked.

It was an Olive thing to say, a bad joke she would have whispered over the com, something that would get them all to chill. "Desperate times call for desperate measures," she said and sighed. "I know I should be focused on the here and now. I know I should concentrate on us getting out of here, first and

foremost. And I know that they can take care of themselves, but
. . ."

"You're worried." I continued pulling and pushing at the stone. "We're a team. A family that's been looking after each other for these last few years, often through very serious and dangerous shit. That's not a bad thing, Av."

"I'm not supposed to feel—" She cut herself off.

"Feel what?"

"Feel *anything*."

"You're human," I reminded her. "You're allowed to feel things."

"I haven't really felt human for a long time," she whispered. "I don't think I'm capable of it." She felt quiet for a heartbeat. "Look at what I did to you."

I froze, sucked in a breath.

TWELVE

Ava

WHY HAD I SAID THAT?

Oh God, why in the ever-loving fuck had I said that?

"What did you do to me, baby?"

My heart skipped a beat, lungs seizing for a moment. "Don't call me baby."

"What did you do to me, Ava?" A slight emphasis on her name, but no apology for the endearment present.

I let it slide. After all, I was the one with the giant mouth. "Any luck with the rock?"

"What, Ava?" he asked impatiently.

"I—"

What *had* I done? Regretted pushing him away? Yes. Wanted him every moment of the last two years? Double yes. Hated that I'd been a total bitch, even knowing that it was the only way to keep him at a distance? Yes, once again.

And now I'd spent the last ten minutes giving away too much—telling him that I'd been in this fucking cell before, that I'd broken my promise to never be back in it, and worst of all, that I'd done something to him.

"I'm a big boy, sweetheart," he said. "I can handle it."

"Don't call me sweetheart," I snapped. "And you know what? I didn't do anything to you."

"You're right," he told me.

"And even if I did end things rather abruptly between us, it was only for the better of the team. We're not like Laila and Ryker."

"No, we're not."

I listened to the soft scrape of rock against rock. "So, we couldn't have kept on with what we were doing. It would have been bad for everyone."

"Bad for you," he murmured. "Bad for you and those solid walls you have up."

My breath caught. "What?"

"What happened after we flew back that day?"

"I don't know what you're talking about."

"Bullshit." More crunching, the sound of pebbles hitting the ground reaching my ears. "We'd made plans to watch a movie. You'd promised to meet me in my quarters. What happened, *caro*? Why didn't you show?"

Because I'd been reminded of exactly what I was.

One week of fantasy, of fantastic sex, of being more comfortable with another person than I'd ever felt in my life, and I'd thought maybe I could do it, could be with a man, could risk letting someone in.

Then I'd seen the files.

Laila had brought them to me just after Dan and I had returned to headquarters, asking me for insights on another team's mission, promising she'd keep my name out of it, if I'd just offer my opinion on the team's investigation. And . . . I'd seen what my family was doing all over again, remembered precisely what they were capable of.

No, I'd remembered precisely what *I* was capable of.

Not good. Not complete. Not worthy.

A total fucking shredded mess inside.

A person who'd done horrible, horrible things.

I couldn't bring that into anyone's life. Into *his* life.

So, I'd done the only thing I could.

I'd made sure he'd leave me alone.

"I'm not *caro* either."

"Ava."

"It doesn't matter," I said, pushing that day, the pictures, the memories away. This was nearly impossible, of course, considering where I was, but it was what I did. Lock everything down. Move forward. Forget. *Forget.* Forget that I was forgetting.

If you're so good at forgetting, why isn't that week with Dan a long-ago memory? my inner critic countered.

"And then when I came to see you, you were . . . hurting," he said softly. "You wouldn't let me help. Why?"

"I'm not discussing this. We need to figure out our exit. My ankle—"

"Isn't going to get better in the next few minutes or hours," he said. "We're sitting in the dark, and I'm wiggling a rock. Tell me."

"This is an old castle," I said. "The walls are thick. They had a hell of a time wiring it for electricity and WiFi, even on the top story. The signal on our trackers—"

"Isn't that why I'm wiggling the rock?" he asked. "Now, we're trapped here. We're not going anywhere in the next little while, so why don't you tell me why you have those shadows in your eyes?"

Irritation prickled through me. "My eyes are none of your fucking business."

"No," he said. "They're not. But I want to make it my business. Won't you let me in?"

No.

I couldn't let him in. Otherwise he'd see. Otherwise he'd know, and he wouldn't look at me the same way. The soft would be edged out of his eyes and disgust would take its place.

I couldn't have him look at me with disgust.

I just . . . couldn't.

"Ava," he warned.

"I'm not a woman you can push," I muttered.

"I don't want to push you," he said. "I want to *know* you. I want to see what's in your heart, to understand the things that make you happy, make you sad. I—Ava, what I feel for you . . . it's unlike what I've ever felt for anyone else." He inhaled and exhaled slowly. "I *care* about you."

Those words shouldn't warm me.

They should send me running.

Except, this time I couldn't lock myself in my room. It wasn't as simple as skipping a movie date or even as heart-wrenching as threatening to switch teams.

I was trapped in a cell with a man I hadn't been able to stop thinking about for years, one who every time I came in close contact with, made me want to forget all about why I had the barriers in the first place.

Not so much as to protect me.

But to protect him.

"You shouldn't, Dan," I whispered. "You should forget me and move on to someone nice, someone innocent and sweet and lovely, whose worst flaw is that she bites her nails or leaves her socks on the floor."

"I abhor when people bite their nails."

I groaned. "That's not the point."

"Then what *is* the point?"

A sigh, my words sharp. "My point is that you need someone who can open her heart."

"And where am I supposed to find this lovely, sweet, innocent woman who opens up her heart to me and shows me all of that nail-biting and sock-leaving?" he asked.

"Not with me."

The noise of scraping stopped and a few seconds later his voice was very close to my ear. "Don't you see?"

I shivered. "What?"

"Don't you see if I don't find that with you, I won't find it with anyone?"

"Except . . . I can't be the person you want."

"I don't need you to be anyone other than yourself."

It was impossible.

But he didn't know that. Because . . . he didn't know what I'd done.

THIRTEEN

Southern Italy
Unknown hrs local time

Dan

I TOUCHED HER CHEEK.

"Don't," she whispered. "Don't touch me."

I pulled back. "Because you don't want me to? Or because you do?"

"We need to deal with the tracker," she said in a tone bordering on desperate. "Not worry about what I want or don't want."

Shuffling back to the wall because I knew she was right but not letting the thread of conversation drop because we were stuck in this place. We were trapped and probably fucked, tracker or not. And I wanted to know . . .

If she wanted me to touch her.

"What are you afraid to tell me?" I asked.

"I'm not afraid of anything."

Silence.

I went back to work on the rock as I waited her out.

"I'm not."

Continuing to scrape at the loosening edge of the rock, I waited. Probably, it was stupid to try and outwait a sniper, one who could be so still and patient, but this wasn't the normal Ava. She was more open than I had seen her in years, freer, rawer—

Which doubled down on my asshole gene.

Because I was demanding information when she was hurt and dealing with that raw and—

"I haven't talked to my parents for more than five minutes in the past two years," I told her, finally understanding that I needed to give, too. That I was asking her to be vulnerable and to share painful truths, and she needed me to be just as open as her. "I talk to Brit regularly, and I talk to my best friend, Blane." Then I admitted something that made me feel guilty, "And . . . I talk to Blane's mom more often than my own. I tell Allison about my life—as much as I'm able. I know I can go to her for advice, that I can just relax and be myself and know she's just happy to hear from me and shoot the shit."

Her voice was soft. "I'm glad you have that."

I was, too, and I felt really lucky, considering how detached my biological parents were to have that sounding board, to have solid and stable people in my life who didn't keep me at a distance, even though I was rarely available for more than the odd phone call.

"But I feel like a fucking asshole," I said, "knowing that I can talk to her about almost everything when I can't even move the conversation past weather with my own mom." A beat. "Which, I understand, makes me sound like a big whiny baby when I was lucky to grow up in a stable home, to have a roof over my head."

"Dan," Ava said. "That's not your fault. "

"Whose then?" I asked.

"Theirs," she told him. "Just because they made sure you had food and a place to sleep doesn't mean they gave you everything you needed to thrive." I heard her shifting, felt her gaze on me. "You're allowed to have your feelings, to wish you had something different."

"Maybe." I glanced over at her, unable to discern much of her body in the shadows. "But I know how lucky I was, especially when I've seen what other people go through, what you've endured."

"I'm not a victim," she declared.

"Certainly not anymore," I said. "But at one time, you were a victim of your circumstances, just like we all are."

"That's—"

"The truth," I pressed. "The only difference between you and other people is that you've overcome your past."

"Fucking hell, Dan," she burst out. "Do you really want to know? *Do you?*"

"No!" I exclaimed, surprising myself. "I don't want to know or need to know. But it's bothering *you*. It took you away from me when I thought we were at the beginning of something special." I yanked at the fucking rock. "So *yes,* I think I *have* to know. You *have* to tell me. Otherwise—"

"I'm not *ever* going to be open for a relationship, you infuriating man."

"Well, I'm not *ever* going to want anyone but you."

Her inhale was sharp. "What?"

"I—"

I broke off.

Because footsteps were echoing outside the cell.

I launched myself over to her, reached Ava's side the instant the door was wrenched open.

Light blinded me, hands reached in and grabbed hold of me.

"Dan!" Ava called. I felt her fingers brush mine, trying and failing to hold on. I was yanked out of the cell, too many rough hands restraining me to fight off every single one.

Then the door slammed closed.

And I was dragged down the hall of a dungeon belonging to an Italian mafia boss.

FOURTEEN

Ava

I LURCHED UP, throwing myself toward the door, but I didn't make it in time.

The metal panel slammed, and I fell to the ground, the momentary adrenaline disappearing in an instant of agony, my ankle screaming, my side sending fiery pain along my torso.

"Fuck," I whispered, tears prickling. "*Fuck.*"

For a few moments, I concentrated simply on breathing through the hurt, on waiting until my eyes adjusted. They'd been blinded by the light in the hall, by the tears—from my injuries, and not because I was feeling helpless and alone.

Right.

Once I'd calmed and my nerves didn't feel like someone had taken a blowtorch to them, I shifted to the cell door. It was locked, no surprise, but I'd had to try on the off chance that they'd not latched it properly.

I looked through the tiny crack at the bottom of the door, so narrow that hardly any light made it through, but enough that I could lie flat and squint out of it.

Empty, from what I could see.

Empty, from what I could hear.

"Fuck," I whispered again, rolling to my back.

Alone. Dan taken who knew where. They would most certainly hurt him. The question was simply how badly.

I had to get the tracker out.

Now.

Painfully, I crawled my way across the cell, over to the far wall, to the spot where Dan had been working on the rock.

And then I got to work . . .

Scratching away the buildup around the rock I'd managed to remove years before. It loosened and fell to the ground much easier than long ago. But it *had* also been more than a decade. There was dirt and dust crammed around the sliver of stone and it had to be slowly removed, chipped away with calloused fingertips and short nails.

Slow and steady.

Bit by bit.

Just like before.

I'd spent hour after hour doing this before I'd escaped, lying flat like I was now, body riddled with more severe injuries than I was sporting now.

Broken fingers and ribs. Cuts from sharp knives that had dripped my blood onto the stone-covered floor. Bruises and eyes swollen shut.

And I'd still always crawled my way to this wall, this rock.

There was a reason I'd begun working at this particular stone—yes, it stuck out of the wall, but it was also low to the ground. Oftentimes, I'd not been able to do much more than lie down.

And scratch.

And chip away at the old mortar, the dirt and dust that sealed that rock in place.

Until it had finally given way.

Until I'd seen the sliver of the Mediterranean Sea and promised myself that once I escaped, I would never be back in this cell.

"Well, here I am," I whispered. "Back in this fucking nightmare." Even as the one person I'd never wanted tangled up with my family was right in the fucking web and probably being tortured right at this instant.

The hot tear sliding down my cheek surprised me.

Then it pissed me off, made me scratch faster.

Tears didn't help. Not now, not ever.

Instead, I continued doing the single thing that might very well mean the difference between us surviving this place and us dying in the fucking dark.

I scratched until my fingers bled.

FIFTEEN

Dan

THE PUNCH to my ribs took my breath away, sending red-hot pain radiating through me.

Not cracked.

But damn well bruised.

"Tell me," the man I recognized from the elevator demanded. Not one of the goons, though they were lined up like three little ducks against the far wall. Instead, it was Ava's uncle, Fabio, who was speaking, and he wasn't pretending to be charming at the moment, wasn't discussing romance or honeymoons. Rather, he tossed a heavy set of brass knuckles that had just become familiar with my ribs down onto a scarred wooden table.

"Not sure what you're talking about," I said once the pain faded.

"What do you know?" he growled.

"I know a lot of things," I said, already bracing myself for the hurt that was about to come my way. "Like the amount of product in your hair is actually flammable."

The blow across my cheek was expected, splitting my lip, coating my tongue in blood.

The smartass remark was certainly unnecessary, but I'd gone through counter-torture training, had been in a handful of "fun" occasions like this, and in my experience, the best way for me to get out of these situations alive was to keep the snark flowing.

They certainly wouldn't keep me alive if I just gave them what they wanted.

And they definitely wouldn't stop the pain just because I told them the truth.

I was fucked unless KTS could get us out, and my only goal at this moment had to be keeping me and Ava alive until the calvary arrived.

Fingers gripped my hair harshly, yanked my head back until I was forced to meet angry brown eyes that were nearly identical to Ava's. Except, the woman I loved had speckles of gold and green in her irises, flashes of color that were brought out depending on the light of the room, the clothes she was wearing.

"What do you know about the shipments?" Fabio gritted, fingers tightening.

"Did your truckload of lingerie go missing?" I shrugged. "Perhaps it was hijacked somewhere along the way?"

Another blow.

More blood on my tongue.

"What did KTS see?"

My lips curved up. "Everything."

The grip on my hair disappeared, but the relief was only there for a second. Because Fabio stepped back, inclined his head at one of the men on the wall, a giant hulking fucker who stepped forward all too gleefully.

He cracked his knuckles as Fabio headed to the door, saying something sharp in Italian.

The only words I recognized were Ava and cell.

And that made ice fill my veins, worry for Ava blustering forward. Would they take her next? Were they going to her right now?

But before I could open my mouth, say something to delay Fabio from leaving, the hulking fucker closed the distance between us and punched me right in the stomach, stealing my breath, stoppering up the words.

Stopping me from speaking.

Then the door was closed, and Fabio was gone and—

The fists kept coming.

SIXTEEN

Southern Italy
Unknown hrs local time

Ava

THE FIRST SLIVER of light had my hand dropping to my side, my aching fingers flexing, and my breathing evening out.

Just a bit more and—

Footsteps.

Carefully sitting up, the action causing the wound on my side to pull painfully, I covered that tiny opening and focused my gaze on the door.

It wrenched open, and I closed my eyes, not wanting to be blinded, even as the light flared behind my lids. I carefully slit them open, saw the outline of the door, and braced myself to be taken like Dan had been.

Instead, he was shoved through, his body hitting the floor like a sack of bricks.

I forced myself to not react, to stay where I was.

If they wanted to interrogate me, I was going to make sure

Dan was okay first. In the end, I wasn't given a choice in the matter of whether I was staying or going. The door slammed closed, darkness falling over us, the footsteps retreated, and we were alone.

"Dan?" I whispered.

"I'm fine," he said and groaned softly.

"I think we need to both wipe that particular phrase from our vernacular."

A soft chuckle that was trailed by a pained breath. "I'm really okay," he said. "Bruised ribs, split lip. I'll have a shiner, but that's the extent of it."

So, they hadn't gotten really impatient yet.

They were confident in their castle, in their dungeon, in their having swiped two KTS agents from a hotel under full surveillance, and they weren't in a hurry for information. They would wait, would be patient.

Would play.

I forced myself not to shudder and carefully shifted, getting to work on the rock again.

"Let me," Dan said, crawling over and nudging me gently out of the way. "You need to elevate that ankle."

"You're—"

"Bruised, but okay," he said. "I promise. Take a break. I'll work on the corner you got open."

My protest was on the tip of my tongue, but I was already feeling dizzy, so I shifted to the side, giving him space to work, before lying down on my back and staring up at the ceiling. The light coming in from the corner of the stone I'd unearthed was dim, speaking of either dusk or dawn.

It was hard to track the hours.

And I'd been unconscious for part of the trip from the hotel, waking up as they'd carried me down into this fucking dungeon, so while I knew we were on my father's estate, I didn't know if we'd come straight here, or if there had been any detours taken.

If it had been me doing the taking, I would have hauled ass here, gotten us locked up securely, not dilly-dallied on the way.

Which was why I suspected it was dawn.

Well, that and the blood loss.

If I'd been bleeding for a full day as I'd been when I'd woken, I would be dead.

Yay for job skills.

I could tell how many hours had passed by counting the steady *drip-drip* of my life force leaving my body.

And me calling blood my life force?

That told me enough about the state of my body.

I wouldn't live if this escapade dragged on for days, even with the fancy first aid kit from KTS.

The small sliver of light grew as I stared up at the ceiling and contemplated my thoughts. I'd begged for death many times while in this cell, wished for it, wanted it, until I'd finally found the strength and fury to fight for my freedom.

Today that anger was still pulsing through me.

But today, I also had the smallest worry that it might not be enough.

And that worry loosened my tongue.

"I was one of them."

The scrapping stopped, and for a long moment, the only sound was the two of us breathing.

Then Dan spoke. "You grew up with them, Tiger."

I froze, the nickname throwing me off for a moment, but I decided to ignore it. Because I was torn between feeling two things. One, worry and relief tangling in my heart—worry that he would be disgusted when he found out the truth and relief that he'd finally know the truth and so would finally stop, would finally leave . . . before I gave in and confessed how much I wanted him. Two, and this voice was getting louder, blocking out all the fears that had kept me so locked down, that I would tell him and he would understand, and I could maybe, fucking *maybe* live like a normal person.

To stop living this half-life.

To maybe have something more.

Because being back in this cell showed me one thing.

My life over the last decade was knowing that I could never be normal or good. That I was too broken and had done too many bad things to ever have any hope of something real. But was that how I truly felt?

Or was that—as I was starting to suspect—my fear preventing me from getting too close to someone and ending up back in a fucking cell.

Not this cell.

I'd never imagined that was a possibility.

But the truth was that I was already in a cell. A cell *I'd* created.

So, I was going to tell him. He'd probably look on me in disgust, and the truth of who I was would certainly send him running. But at least I would finally be out of my personal prison.

Of course, all of this was slightly easier to bear because we would probably die in this dungeon.

One perk to confinement and torture?

No long-term worrying about the consequences of my actions.

Because death was imminent.

Not that I was giving up. I would fight tooth and nail to the end, but I also understood that the deck was stacked against us, that it wouldn't be a fair fight, and that unless KTS managed to track us down, our chances of getting out weren't great.

All of this had me lifting my chin, releasing a deep breath, and saying, "By one of them, I mean that for the first sixteen years of my life, I lived and breathed the Toscalo life. I hurt people, and I didn't care. I—" Shame washed over me. "I wanted what I wanted. I relished the power. I *enjoyed* it when someone was punished because of some perceived slight to me."

"What happened when you turned sixteen?"

My eyes burned, that shame a heavy burden. "They hurt someone I actually cared about."

"Who?"

"My nanny." I shook my head. "It was silly to still be close to my nanny, especially at sixteen, but my mother wasn't involved in my life except for the odd comment about the way I dressed or how I wore my hair."

"Your father, though," Dan murmured. "He wanted to make you his heir."

Heir to a sick and twisted empire.

"Yes," I said. "I was the oldest and always his favorite. The way he always told it is that he'd say he knew exactly how smart I was going to be from the moment I opened my eyes as a newborn and glared at him. I was a precocious child with a fiery temper, and my father relished that in me."

"And then you grew up."

"I did very well in school. Much better than my younger brothers and so, by the time we were all in double-digits, there was no doubt I would be taking over the Toscalo name." I shook my head. "My father didn't care that I was a woman. He only cared about three things: power, ruthlessness, and money. I'd proven I cared about only the same by the time I was ten."

A long pause.

Then "How?"

I blew out a breath, closed my eyes. "Want to know what it's like to grow up with a child who is given every advantage but rarely told no?" My laugh was brittle. "I can tell you. It's not pretty. If someone teased me, I wouldn't tease back or get mad or even hit them. No, I would find the one toy or possession that was most precious to them, and I would either destroy it and return the broken pieces . . ." The memories of my brother's favorite truck, my so-called best friend's favorite doll, and how I'd relished breaking them flashed through my mind. "Or, as I got older and was better able to control myself, I would ransom it back."

"Ava."

I ignored him. "And my father was so proud of me. He couldn't stop talking about how ingenious and ruthless I was. He encouraged me, and I fucking loved doing it."

"Until something happened with your nanny."

"Yes."

"What, honey? What happened?"

"I caught her stealing, and—" I broke off. "I—"

He waited, and I pushed through the shame.

"I was the one who hurt her."

The sharp inhalation had my heart sinking. Then his voice was gentle, *too* gentle. "I'm sure that's not everything."

"Don't be nice," I said. "It was my fault. I reported her to my father. And h-he made me—" Horror washed over me, like I was in that room all over again. Like I was the one lifting the blade, bringing it down over Isa's hand. "No. I could have stopped it. I should have stopped it."

Dan came over to me, took my hand. "Should have stopped what?"

"I should have stopped him from cutting off her hand!" I swallowed the bile that rose in my throat. The memory of the blade slicing through skin, getting stuck on the bone, Isa's cries of pain made me physically sick, but not more than the fact that *I'd* done it. I was the reason she'd been in that room. I should have . . . done so many things differently, not the least of which was to not report the one person who'd shown me kindness without manipulation, without strings. I'd known my father had hated thieves, knew he punished them severely.

And I'd still reported her.

She'd taken forty dollars, and not even for herself. Isa had mailed that money to her son, so he could buy food for his family.

"Did you know what was going to happen?"

"I—"

A finger on my lips. "I'm not trying to be an asshole here, Ava. But stop and think. Would anything have been different if you hadn't told?"

I hesitated. "Yes."

"What would have changed?"

"*Everything*," I said. "*I* wouldn't have been the one who caused her to get hurt, for one. If I hadn't reported her, she would have—" I clenched my jaw, forced myself to release it. "She would have been whole, and I wouldn't have been like them."

"And did you want them to do it?"

My eyes flew to his. "Of course not. I loved Isa, and I-I—" Voice breaking, I took a deep breath. "But it doesn't matter what I wanted or what I wish could have changed." Because I had done it, and Isa had been hurt, and it had been because of me. "This was my fault, and I'll never forgive myself for it, for not understanding the consequences of what I was doing, for not refusing to do it in the first place."

"Everyone has regrets," he whispered. "Things they wished they did differently."

"And what are your regrets?"

"You know my biggest one," he said. "I told you about it in Georgia."

My lungs froze. "The mission in Syria."

"Yes." The word was filled with pain. "We missed the target, and he ended up killing his entire family." He cleared his throat. "Those kinds of regrets haunt people like us, make us have nightmares about what we could have done differently. But that doesn't mean that—"

"I'm a bad person?" I shook my head. "Of course, it does. I hurt my friends, my siblings. The people who cared about me. I betrayed them like it was as easy as it was to change a pair of socks."

"Until you understood exactly what it meant."

I stopped, considered that. Considered that he might be right. Except . . . that was too easy, too pat an excuse. "No," I said. "What I have is confirmation that I'm *exactly* like them."

"Ava."

"Do you know how I know that?" I asked, talking over him. "Why I didn't meet you for that date two years ago?" I released a shaky breath when I saw him shake his head. "Because when I got back to headquarters, Laila asked me to look at some files. And you know what was in those?"

"No, honey."

I barely heard the endearment, not when there were so many other important things to focus on. Like my DNA. Like the fact that I'd done unforgivable things. Like the fact that I'd always have these deeds hanging over me and couldn't ever forgive myself.

"The files had pictures of body parts. Fingers, hands, ears that were branded with a T." Bile burned the back of my throat. "Parts that my family had removed and delivered to people as threats."

"Oh, baby."

"No," I whispered. "Enough with the endearments and the soft tones. It was the reminder I needed then. It's the reminder I need now." I shook off his hand, knowing that my thoughts earlier about being different had been sentimental tripe. I wasn't different. Wouldn't ever be different. "I'll never be like you, Dan." Even if part of me deep down wished he wouldn't push me away, wished I could pretend to be normal and a woman he could be with, the rest of me knew that wasn't ever going to happen.

I'd done awful things.

I'd hurt the people who cared for me.

I—

"You were a child."

"That doesn't make it okay!" I exclaimed. "I knew it was wrong, and I did all of it anyway. And worse, Isa never hated me. She should have. Should have despised me for what I'd done." My eyes burned. "Instead, she came to my room that night, comforted *me*. How fucked up is that?"

"Because *you were a child.*"

"I was sixteen. That's an adult in plenty of places in the world." I reached up and shoved my hair out of my face. "I didn't grow up like you, Dan, didn't have a wonderful sister and normal parents. I'm not saying they were great, that they gave you everything you needed . . ." I remembered how he'd felt left alone, like they'd disengaged from his and his sister's lives. But—

"But they didn't make their living exploiting others."

"Yes." I sighed. "And that's *all* I know. That's the bread and butter I was raised on."

A brief blip of silence.

"And there is nothing I can say to you that will make this okay. Nothing that will excuse your actions."

Even though I knew it was the truth, hearing him say that out loud was a blow.

"Exactly," I whispered.

"So, the only thing I *can* tell you is that this is all fucking bullshit."

SEVENTEEN

Southern Italy
Unknown hrs local time

Dan

"WHAT?" she whispered.

"It's all bullshit," I said. "Yes, your childhood was fucked up. But no, you're not a product of that. Once you understood, you fought." I covered her hand with mine. "You told me that yourself. You told me that you spent too many days in this cell. You told me that you got out and now you put your life on the line for innocent people every day. You do good."

"No, I want to pretend I'm good. But *that's* the bullshit."

"Ava—"

"Go back to the fucking wall. It was a mistake telling you any of this."

"Ava—"

"Cut the emotional horseshit, and let's focus on getting out of here alive."

"I didn't take you for a coward."

"What?"

Irritated by her obstinance, I made my way over to the wall, digging my fingers into the dirt and succeeding in wiggling the rock. "This is all very convenient. Your horrible past means that you don't have to get close to anyone, that you can keep us all at a distance." I yanked harder. "You're too scared of getting close, too scared you might hurt someone. Except . . . that's life. People hurt other people. Not usually on purpose, but I don't think a lot of what you did was on purpose—"

"I just told you that I—"

"You were a sixteen-year-old girl who was in an untenable situation, who was raised by an unbelievably manipulative and violent father to do horrible things. *That* was the unforgivable part. *He* did that to you." I forced myself to pause, to moderate my tone. "What is admirable is that you realized what was going on and that you found some good even amongst all this darkness."

She scoffed. "That's all a pat story. But it doesn't absolve me of my part in all I did."

"No," I said. "But I think what's more pat is you using this fear and the walls to keep people out because you're afraid they may hurt *you*. Because as much as you want to pretend it's you protecting the world from your evilness, it's really about you protecting yourself from anyone who might get close enough to betray you."

I heard her inhale sharply.

"That's not—" She broke off, fell silent.

I let her think as I continued working on the wall, feeling very much like Sisyphus and his proverbial rock, only instead of rolling it up a hill, I was trying to pull it loose from ten years of dirt and grime.

"I might have gotten out," she whispered after an interminable silence. "But I didn't come out whole. I don't think I'll ever be able to make right what I did."

"You can't change what happened."

"What? You going to advise me to put my past behind me and move forward?"

"Yes."

"And have you forgotten Syria?"

"No," I said. "And I won't *ever* forget it, but that's not the obstacle that's preventing me from moving forward. Rather, it's the building block for my blueprint of *how* to move forward." I shook my head. "I will regret how that mission went down for the rest of my life, but I've taken those mistakes, I've made certain that I won't ever make the same ones again."

"It's not that easy."

I froze. "Did I say it was easy?" A beat. "Some days it's the hardest fucking thing to do, moving forward, not letting my regrets hold me back." A big chunk of the compacted dirt came off in my hands. "And you know who taught me that?"

"No."

"Brit," I said. "My sister is the most fearless person I know. Bad shit happened to her, but even if I put that aside, and I look at all the ways people tried to hold her back, opportunities were given to her with strings and taken away as easily as breathing. And she spent *years* with a target on her back." I swallowed as the fury at what my little sister had been through, things I hadn't been able to protect her from pushed forward. That was another one of those regrets that had become a building block, another reason I was at KTS trying to make the world a better place. "She's lucky in so many ways, for sure, but she struggled, she pushed back, and she didn't let past regrets stop her. I'm supposed to be the older brother, but it's me being so damned proud of her, seeing her live her life and grab hold of the things she wanted that's made me realize I can't keep looking backward."

When Ava didn't say anything, I decided to lay my final card on the table. "And the person I want to look forward with is you. It's *always* been you."

Quiet. Long, drawn out, uncomfortable quiet.

Then soft, *soft* words. "I won't ever be capable of a normal relationship."

Continuing to brush the dirt away, I felt the rock give a little bit. "You're capable of a lot more than you realize, sweetheart."

More silence.

"And for the record, I don't give a shit about normal," I told her. "I just want you to be you."

"Dan," she sighed.

"No decisions while we're in a cell," I said.

"When should I make said decisions?"

"Once we're out of here and safe."

"Dan."

"Ava."

Another long moment of quiet. "Okay. Once we've made it out of here alive, I'll think about what you said." I breathed a sigh of relief. At least until she spoke again, her voice tinged with sharp. "Did you just call me sweetheart again?"

Fuck. "It slipped out," I said. "Just pretend I complimented you on your superior sniper abilities and forget all use of endearments."

"*Dan.*"

I focused on the wall. "I've almost got the stone out."

"You're a pain in my ass," she muttered.

Since I knew the time for serious conversations had passed —for the moment, at least—I went for a joke. "And once again, you're agreeing with my sister."

She laughed quietly then groaned and grabbed her side. "Stop being funny."

"It's a gift. I can't just stop out of nowhere." And then—*yes!* I managed to get my finger behind that sliver of rock and began to coax it out.

It came, millimeter by millimeter.

Finally, it was free, light pouring into the space. I glanced through quickly, saw enough to assess that Ava was right in that we were still near the Mediterranean. More than that was difficult to discern, so I leaned back and used the light to make my way back to her, to assess her injuries.

"We need to cut the tracker out," she said, holding up her arm and exposing the inside of her elbow to the light, where the small GPS chip was located. "We can use the underwire of my bra. Sharpen it against the rocks—"

"Wait, Ava." No fucking way was I cutting into her skin. We did need to cut the tracker out, but it would be out of my damn arm. "I need to see that ankle."

"That's—"

"I need you in fighting shape," I said. "If we're going to get out of here, yeah?"

"I'm—"

"That's the truth, yeah? I can't fight to get us out and have to haul your ass out of here."

"Stop interrupting me."

"Then focus and stop being stubborn." My tone was deliberately sharp, hoping to make her mad, hoping that the slight lacing of panic and fear still threading through her tone would disappear under a deluge of angry. Because when Ava got angry, she was the most dangerous enemy someone could face.

And because if Ava was angry, she wouldn't be that little girl, scared and trapped in this cell again.

"Do I need to call you sweetheart again?"

She scowled. "Do I need to call you *asshole?*"

"If that gets you out of that boot and splinted up sooner then, yes."

"I'm not taking this boot off. If I do, it's going to swell up, and then I really won't be able to do shit on it." I wasn't sure I agreed with her, but I *was* pretty certain that I needed to see the knife wound that was supposedly *not* serious on her abdomen.

"Fine," I said.

"Fine?"

"Yup. Let's move on." I reached for the hem of her T-shirt, tugged it up, and—"Fuck, Ava. This isn't a bit of blood." The emergency bandage was soaked through, even with KTS's special clotting solution. Dried blood coated her abdomen, and the white material of the binding was bright red.

"Maybe it's more than a bit," she said. "But there's nothing to be done for it."

"And how about your arm?" I asked. "Is that really a graze?"

She tugged up the sleeve of her shirt. "Yes," she muttered, showing me the bright red gouge on her left triceps. "Just a graze. Thankfully, I moved fast enough to at least avoid that."

I studied the mark, debated for a moment at retrieving my own medical kit for the knife wound, but knew we might need it later.

It was better to conserve resources.

Especially, if the rest of the team was in the same position as us.

Right then. On to the next thing. Reaching for my belt buckle, I yanked it out of its loops.

"Um," Ava began. "What are you doing?"

I undid the button, tugged down the zipper.

"Getting naked."

EIGHTEEN

Southern Italy
Unknown hrs local time

Ava

"GETTING NAKED?" I asked.

More like squawked, but that was mostly because he'd sprawled on his back and was shoving his pants down his legs.

"Seriously, Dan. What in the fuck are you doing?"

He reached into the front of his boxer briefs, and I slammed my eyes closed. Why in the fuck was I slamming my eyes closed? I'd seen it, and I'd loved it, and I wanted to get my hands and mouth and tongue all over it again—

But by the time I managed to open my eyes again, his hand was out, his pants were coming back up, and he was tossing a small package my way.

I caught it reflexively then winced, remembering just where his hand had been.

"New from the tech squad," he said. "Small blade in the hem of my boxers. You'll have to open it up though. Fred"—the man back at main headquarters who designed a lot of our equipment—"just threw it in at the last minute. I swear, he used duct tape and superglue."

Lifting it up so I could see the small silver package, wrapped in what indeed looked like duct tape, I began working at the seam.

With my teeth.

Probably, I should have been grossed out.

But frankly, I'd had my mouth in worse places, and . . . also I didn't consider Dan's cock a *worse place*.

Glorious, maybe.

Ugh.

Enough.

No decisions in this cell. Even if his words, his lack of disgust had me wrangling with what I'd always thought was the truth about who I was.

Eventually, I got the edge on the package open and was unpeeling the tape. "This is far below Fred's usual standards."

Dan buttoned his pants, yanked up the zipper. "He's trying to figure out the safest mode of blade transport. It's more difficult than the sole of a shoe, putting it in a waistband or hem of a piece of clothing."

"You don't want to stab yourself trying to get it out."

"Right," he said. "Or just walking around."

"But it needs to be small and relatively undetectable, especially during a potential pat-down." I slanted a glance at him "Is this where you tell me that your junk is so big, and that's why they didn't find it?"

A snort. "Not hardly." His eyes flitted up, a cocky smile curving his mouth. "Although, this *could* be the point where I say you've seen it and . . ."

"It's tiny?"

He mimed like I wounded him.

"Stop." I smacked him lightly, kept unwrapping, even as I considered our options. The first thing I'd done when I'd woken up in the back of the van transporting us was to check our supplies. I'd run through our resources, painfully bound my wound in the back of the moving vehicle, checked that Dan was breathing. It hadn't taken long to discover that all of our weapons had been taken.

Luna.

Poor Luna was probably tossed in the trash or the water somewhere, never to be used again.

I spared a moment for my poor rifle, most certainly discarded like a broken toy in some sad, dark place, and focused on getting out of here. "They knew about the blades in our boots, but not the first aid kits."

"Or the underwear knives."

I shuddered. "That's *not* the name to call them."

"Point made," he said. "And taken."

"Aside from bad word usage, they knew our room, and I'm guessing they also knew also about the surveillance, otherwise we would have seen them coming on the cameras."

"Do you think they hacked it?"

I sighed, pulled the tiny knife from the plastic wrapping, and handed it to Dan. "I don't know. But they would've *had* to, right? Either that, or we have another—" Breaking off, because I didn't want to finish the sentence, I just shook my head.

He didn't have that problem. "Traitor."

"Right." The question was, "Is this one new or the one we already know about?"

A nod. "Exactly."

KTS didn't exist in a vacuum. We'd had traitors before, those who gave in to the temptation of power or money. Daniel —the former agent we'd connected to criminal activity—was one of those. He had betrayed us barely a year before, and the memory was fresh enough that it seemed like the most likely scenario.

"Do you think Daniel"—it was a cruel twist that Dan shared a name with the bastard—"was a part of this?" I asked.

Laila had come face-to-face with Daniel on a mission not long ago—just months after the former agent had betrayed KTS and their team for the money and power offered by the Mikhailova clan. That betrayal had been a particular blow because Daniel had been previously fired by the agency, and Laila had vouched for her childhood friend to come back as a member of her team on a probational basis. He'd abused that trust then attempted to steal the drives KTS had recovered, putting two civilians' lives at risk.

It was a fucked-up move, from a fucked-up person.

A person who—if he was somehow alive—was out there now with information about KTS.

Information he was potentially—and in all likelihood—sharing with their enemies.

We all understood why the Mikhailova—and as a consequence, Daniel—wanted the drives. They had contained information linking the Russians with many powerful people around the world, and the trail of money had given KTS rare insight into the inner workings of the Mikhailova. In fact, a whole team at KTS was currently working on cutting off those monetary channels to make their criminal activities more difficult.

But in the aftermath of that most recent interaction with Laila, Daniel had been presumed dead by her hand. Except . . . KTS trained their people to be strong, to never give up, and gave them numerous techniques to get out of a variety of sticky situations.

I wasn't at all certain that a knife wound and subsequent explosion could take him down permanently.

I was still kicking.

Though the jury was out for how long.

Adrenaline was getting me through, but I knew that was a limited resource. At some point, my body would either succumb to infection or lose too much blood and be unable to function. Add in the ankle and Dan's multitude of injuries and . . .

Yeah, I was still kicking.

And the question still was: for how long?

"Frankly," I said, "this whole situation—our mission being hijacked, my father's people knowing exactly where to find us and when to take us down, along with the previous meet with our source going FUBAR—suggests that Daniel might very much be alive."

"Seems likely he survived the incident at the warehouse with Laila and that he's behind this," Dan agreed. "He knew how to get to us. And he knew about our old tech, but not the newly issued stuff."

My ankle and side had both been slowly ratcheting up with pain, a steady *throb-throb-throb* that was building as time went on.

Adrenaline fading.

Ignoring that, I lay back, trying to pretend the pain wasn't there. "Right. The first aid kits have only been common in the last few months, and the knife is new even to me." I closed my eyes, attempted to breathe through the hurt. "But this mission hasn't been on the books anywhere Daniel could have known about it. We planned it in a week."

"If he's alive and working with them," Dan pointed out, "he could have spotted our setup."

"That's true." I opened my eyes.

"Either way, we'll have to change tactics in the future," he said.

"Agreed." A beat as I tilted my head, staring up at him. "Could he have known about our source in Munich?"

Dan nodded. "That's possible, especially since he'd been reinstated to Laila's team for a time. That source had been around for a while."

The puzzle pieces were fitting together, and I didn't like one bit where this was leading. But we would have time to talk after we got out of this cell. And step one of that was ensuring our trackers were able to be picked up by KTS's servers.

I lifted my arm. "Take it out."

Instead of listening to me, Dan lifted his own arm and sliced the spot just on the inside of his elbow. He hissed in pain, and I glared as blood dripped out of the open wound.

"Why'd you do that?" I exclaimed. "I'm the injured one. It doesn't make sense to weaken the stronger of us."

He rolled his eyes, pressing at his skin until he managed to remove the grain-sized implant. "The day I get taken down by a tiny wound is the day I turn in my agent card."

"It makes no sense—"

Dan tore a strip from his T-shirt and handed it to me. "Tie this for me."

I gestured to his boot. "The kit."

"Let's save that for now."

My brows pulled down. "We—"

"Fine," he said, wrapping it with one hand and bending like he was going to hold it in place with his teeth. "I'll do it myself."

"Fucking stubborn," I muttered, shifting toward him. My side screamed in pain, though it felt like the bleeding had stopped—maybe there was hope for me yet. Still, moving a foot to my right was a hell of a lot easier than when I'd had to bandage myself in the van. It wasn't easy, of course, not with my ankle feeling more like a sausage stuck in its casing with each passing moment.

Part of me was aware that Dan didn't actually need me to tie the strip of cotton. He'd most certainly managed many times over the years. This was his way of keeping me focused and moving and making sure that I continued looking forward.

Sometimes the only thing that got people out of a tough situation was to keep putting one foot in front of the other.

Create a list of tasks.

Accomplish them.

Step 1: remove one of our GPS trackers. Check.

Step 2: get it outside, in case the one remaining in my arm couldn't broadcast its signal through rocks.

I tied off the bandage, making sure it was tight enough that the bleeding would stop as quickly as possible then reclined flat onto the floor to conserve my energy.

"Thanks," Dan murmured, moving to the opening. He shoved his fingers through.

Just as I heard footsteps on the floor.

"They're coming back," I hissed.

He nodded, pulling back and grabbing the sliver of stone and sticking it into place. The space immediately filled with darkness, and I felt my breath catch. Dark. Days in this cell. No one coming to help me. All alone.

His hand wrapped around mine.

And the tight feeling in my lungs eased.

Step 3: find a way to get out of this shithole.

Heart thudding, I handed Dan the small knife. "For when the time comes."

His fingers squeezed mine, and he pocketed it. "We'll get out of here. It'll be fi—"

Optimistic wasn't exactly what I was feeling at this moment, but I wasn't going to waste any more time worrying about the past, about what might happen. I needed to focus on being strong and on thinking about the next step, and—

I needed to live in the fucking present.

Yanking his hand, I tugged him toward me. Dan came,

rolling easily, supporting his weight on his elbows, his body poised over mine.

"What do you need?" he asked.

"Kiss me."

Then, not bothering to wait for his response, I slanted my lips across his.

It was the wrong time. It was stupid and irresponsible behavior for an agent, especially when footsteps were barreling down upon us, when people who wanted to hurt us would be opening that cell door.

But . . . it was also the perfect time.

Because I might not have another opportunity to kiss Dan.

Because I was so fucking tired of not actually living my life.

Because I was terrified that if I remained this broken creature, I would never have anything good.

Only darkness. Forever alone.

There was a tumult inside me, fear driving me to pull back, but that same fear also pushed me to continue moving forward, to believe in his words, to grasp onto this one moment when it may very well be our last.

His mouth was soft, coaxing, his lips parting, his tongue slipping inside my mouth.

Then it was less fear and more need, more want, more *feeling*.

This man had always made me feel good. Just being in the same room with him, discussing mission parameters or actively working a case had always soothed part of the ragged edges inside me. But *this*—touching him, kissing him, feeling the heat of his body surrounding me, his lips on mine, his tongue in my mouth—and it didn't even come close to good. It was nirvana. It was everything. It was—

The cell door creaked, and we pulled apart.

"Light," I warned, shifting up into a crouch—my side burning, my ankle throbbing. But I shoved the pain down, focused on this next step.

Step 4—no, Step 5, because Step 4 had been kissing Dan.

Step 5 was to get out of here.

The door was yanked open, light flaring into the space, burning my eyes. I'd squinted, avoiding the bulk of the light, but it was still impossible for me to not be momentarily blinded.

I knew Dan was in the same boat.

Hands reached in, wrenching me out.

Since *out* was where I wanted, since *out* might get us out of this fucking hell hole, I didn't fight the pull, even when the sharp movements made agony scorch through my body.

Biting my cheek until it bled, I held back the instinctive cry of pain.

The cell door slammed closed.

I looked to my right, my left.

No Dan.

He was alone in the dark.

And I was standing toe-to-toe with my father.

———

I WAS IN THE CHAIR.

Metal cuffs wrapped around my wrists, rough wood against my bare skin, my legs hanging toward the ground, my ankle swelling more by the second.

And my father was going through his routine.

Peeling off his jacket, rolling up his shirt sleeves, turning to face me, and casually crossing his arms over his chest. "I didn't expect us to be back in this place."

I snorted. "Preaching to the choir," I muttered.

Him closing the distance between us and getting in my face wasn't a surprise, neither was the bruising grip on my jaw, the fingers tangling in my hair and yanking my head back.

"I didn't say you could speak."

"I stopped listening to your orders a long time ago."

The fingers tightened, pinpricks of pain dotting my scalp. "Tell me why you are in Italy."

"I was taking a vacation with my boyfriend." I glared up at him. "Congrats for kidnapping two lovebirds on vacation."

Dark brows drawing down, brown eyes sparking with fury.

I braced myself for the blow that was sure to come my way. Instead, he released me, a small smile curving his lips. "Always so much fire inside you, my Eva. Just like all the Toscalos before you. Fury and cruelty are your constant companions."

"That's not my name anymore."

"You can try to deny your heritage, my daughter, but that's all it will be. A denial."

I didn't bother answering. It wasn't like anything I could say would change his mind or convince him to let us go. I'd been in this room before, often and long enough before my eye injury to have counted the stones forming each wall. So, I didn't need my glasses—lost somewhere during the fight or my removal from the hotel—to see that there were two hundred and six rocks on the one directly in front of me, three hundred and eighty-seven on the one to my right, three hundred and twelve to my left, one hundred and ninety-two behind me. All flat chunks of gray stone joined together with mortar, but in a variety of sizes. Not the polished finish of the house above, but older construction from centuries before.

Even old, the stones made for excellent sound-proofing.

I knew.

I'd lived that.

Just as I knew there was a heavy wooden door in the middle of the wall behind me, dark mahogany and scarred from years of use. The knob was heavy and stained black from the years, as hard to turn as the ancient key my father carried around for this purpose.

Just as the cell was my uncle's favorite form of torture—dark, silent, isolated, cramped—this room was my father's.

In another life, the well-lit space could pose as a tasting room at a winery, a long-standing space in some old Tuscan villa. There were even tables and chairs, built-in wooden shelves to hold things. Only, the items they were holding weren't bottles of wine or glasses or corkscrews.

Instead, there were shining rows of knives, different lengths of rope, drills and hammers, scissors, and saws.

Oh, and there was the odd corkscrew.

Just for fun.

"I would like to know how you came to the hotel," my father said, his tone soft. The gentle question didn't fool me. I knew all about this soft and gentle side, knew how he could flip the switch in an instant, turn vicious and as dangerous as a snake.

"I told you," I said. "Vacation."

"With three teams from that useless agency you joined after leaving here."

"I don't know what you're talking about."

One second, he was spinning away from me, his gaze on the racks on the far wall. The next, he'd spun back and his fist was descending toward me.

I flinched back, but realistically, I had nowhere to go. My head hit the back of the chair, and a heartbeat later, his fist collided with my cheek. Here was the weird thing about getting punched in the face. For a moment, I felt nothing. No impact. No pain. Nothing at all. Then my nerves exploded, fire burning through my skin. The force of his fist crunching my skull into the wood of the chair.

I'd like to pretend it was no big deal.

But getting punched, especially in the face, really fucking hurt.

And it was only exasperated by my ankle, by the wound in my side.

Note to self: flinching and gasping in pain didn't mix well with multiple injuries.

"Why were you at the hotel?" he asked again.

"Really great sex."

Another punch, this time to my stomach.

The only lucky part was that he hit the side without the wound. But that didn't mean it wasn't still agony tearing through me. I started bleeding almost immediately, felt it dripping down my side, and I couldn't hold back my cry of pain.

"Oh, I'm sorry, *bella*," he murmured. "Did I hurt you?"

I didn't bother answering. Okay, so maybe I *couldn't* answer. Not when my head was swimming, black teasing at the edges of my vision, not when my breaths were coming in short gasps.

"Tell me how KTS came to know about the hotel!"

I swallowed hard, but I didn't have to swallow the words, didn't struggle to not say anything about my agency, my team, my mission. I'd been through this many times before. I'd passed the counter-torture training with flying colors.

Because my father, my uncle, my brothers, my cousins—they'd all tried to break me.

And they'd failed.

I'd die for KTS in a heartbeat, for what we were doing, to stop my bastard of a father from having any additional information that might help his "business." There was absolutely no doubt of that.

"Why, *bella?*"

Lifting my chin, I said, "I. Like. Sex."

Another punch, more blood trickling down my side.

"Why?"

"I especially like it with hot men."

Fury in cold brown eyes, in the heavy lines of his face. He raised his fist again and said, "You'll—"

A knock at the heavy brown door.

One of my cousins, dressed like the other men in an expensive suit sans tie, his crisp white shirt unbuttoned at his throat, pushed off the wall and walked behind me. I heard the door open, the soft murmur of voices, and then footsteps.

A moment later, he was back in my line of vision, stepping close to my father and murmuring in his ear.

My father's face went blank as his gaze locked on mine.

It's funny. People often associate blank with nothingness. But I knew blank could be so much more. It could hide fear. It could mask longing. It could encase violent anger in a calm façade that was at constant risk of exploding outward.

That was what I knew instinctively had happened in this situation. My father might seem composed and completely unaffected by whatever news had just been whispered in his ear, but I was absolutely certain that was simply an act. I'd been on the receiving end of the explosion more than enough times to understand what was brewing beneath that placid surface.

He nodded once, stepped toward me, gripped my hair.

And I braced.

For the eruption. For the pain. For the Toscalo family special of both.

Only today . . .

That explosion would be happening elsewhere.

Because with one more dark glare, my father let go. "Soon, *bella*. Soon we'll have another conversation," he hissed into my ear. "Or perhaps, I'll have your uncle keep you company while you wait for me to complete my business."

Bile burned the back of my throat, but I forced myself to not shrink away, to not flinch or react.

He nodded at one of my cousins and left the room, the *click-click* of his shoes echoing on the stone floor.

The door shut quietly behind him.

And then I found myself unstrapped from the chair by angry hands, yanked to my feet, and hauled . . .

Not to my uncle. Not for the moment anyway.

But back to my cell.

Back into the darkness and wondering what business had pulled my father away from one of his favorite pastimes.

Torturing me.

NINETEEN

Dan

THE FOOTSTEPS PRECEDED the door opening, and this time I was ready.

I lurched forward, prepared to fight.

Only to have Ava launched into my arms. I stumbled, the crouch I was in due to the low ceiling not helpful in keeping my balance, and though I landed hard on both knees, I did manage to keep hold of her.

She hissed out a breath.

"Okay?" I asked as the cell door slammed and locked shut.

"Honestly," she said between short, little gasped breaths, "I've been better."

Snorting, I carefully set her down then went and yanked the rock out from where I'd hastily stowed it.

"See anything?"

"No," I said. "Though it's definitely morning. Or the end of it anyway. The sun's almost directly overhead."

"Got it."

I moved back over to her, noting the sheen of sweat on her forehead, the paleness of her skin. Lifting her shirt, I saw her wound had bled again, and bruises were beginning to blossom on her torso. Anger flooded through me, but I buried it deep, would use it as motivation to get us the fuck out of here. "I should rewrap this," I told her.

"Yes," she agreed. "But in a little bit. Let me just lay here."

"Your ankle?"

She closed her eyes. "That and the rest of me. I think I need to take it out of the boot, but that's going to make me less mobile."

"Losing feeling?"

A nod.

Shit.

"Rest for a minute," I said. "I'll sort out a splint."

Another nod.

I took off my boot, yanked the bandage out of the tongue, ripped out the insole. I'd use the insert of Ava's, along with her lace to wrap her ankle. But the idea of causing her pain made my skin itch.

I knew she needed it secure, that it was dangerous now if she was losing feeling.

That didn't make what I was about to do any easier.

"Do you remember when we were outside, and out of nowhere it started pouring?" she asked.

My pulse picked up. There was only one time when we'd been together and unprepared for the sudden change in weather. At my cabin in Georgia. The buzz of the insects growing louder, the humidity in the air increasing, until it had suddenly gotten dark.

And the skies had opened up.

We should have run for the house, avoiding most of the soaking rain.

But Ava had sprawled back onto the blanket and smiled like it was the best day of her life.

"I'd never felt rain like that," she murmured. "Never been trapped in a storm when it was so warm out, its cool kiss a relief."

She'd stripped off her shirt, her pants, and eventually her underwear, laughing as the drops had continued to fall, and I'd been mesmerized by her damp skin, the droplets coalescing in her curves and flooding open. She glanced over at me, where I'd jumped up and began gathering our things to run into the house, and crooked a finger.

Suddenly, I hadn't cared about the book I'd been reading or the fact that our lunch was soaked through.

I'd dropped everything and spent the next hour drinking those tiny puddles from her body as I'd kissed my way across every inch of her body.

"I remember," I said, shoving my boot back on and tying it securely.

"I'd never seen rain fall like that before," she murmured. "Clear skies to an absolute downpour in seconds." Her eyes opened. "I think about that week a lot."

"Me, too," I said, moving toward her. "Sometimes it's hard to think about anything else when I'm in the room with you."

A soft laugh. "We were supposed to be done."

"I think that was just the beginning," I said, gently unlacing her boot, gritting my teeth and setting myself about the task, even when she winced. It had to be done. I'd be careful, get it over with as quickly as possible. "I wasn't supposed to be on Laila's team at all, did you know that?"

"No," she whispered.

"I had my own team, was happy with the work we were doing."

"What happened?"

"I saw you."

Her jaw dropped open. "That's insane."

"Maybe," I admitted. "But you and Laila were coming back from a mission. I'd just returned from one with my own team. I'd finally had everything I thought I'd wanted, had been working toward, and yet . . ."

"What?"

"I was empty." I carefully began tugging the boot off. "I saw you and thought you were the most beautiful thing I'd ever seen. And then I talked to you, saw how capable you were—hell, you remember that mission in Paris when both our teams were deployed to cover the ambassador? Our entire cover was almost blown, and then you came in and saved all our asses by pretending to be lost."

She shrugged. "Powerful men like that tend to underestimate women like me."

"A woman like you?"

"Short, average-sized women with average faces."

I touched her cheek. "Or he was struck by a beautiful woman with kind eyes and a good soul." My lips tipped up. "Like I was." She snorted as I brushed a finger over her lips. "Though, I can't lie and say that I wasn't fully aware of the fucking gorgeous curves hidden beneath your uniform, and I swear, I'd be able to pick your ass out of a lineup without issue, I've stared at it so many times."

"You're a pig." A beat. "Also, I think your ass is perfectly squeezable."

I grinned, stifling a laugh. Because seriously, we were trapped in a cell in the creepy-ass dungeon of an Italian mob boss, and I was laughing. "Big words from a woman who is in possession of a perfect specimen herself."

"Such bad game," she said dryly.

"I don't need game," I said, continuing to gently coax the boot from her foot.

"Wh-why's that?" she asked, through a hissed-out breath.

I stopped pulling. "Because what I feel about you isn't a game or some passing attraction. I certainly thought you were gorgeous and liked you before that week in my cabin. Obviously, I respected your abilities and how smart you were. And you know I thought you were a hell of a shot, after all the times I begged you to come with me to the range." She chuckled. "But after that week we spent together, and in the years since, even though our relationship wasn't all I wanted, I still got to know *you*." Another gentle tug. Another wince that tugged at my heart strings. "And the you I know is pretty fucking fabulous."

Ava made a scoffing noise.

"You are." I cupped her cheek with one hand. "Why can you see the good in everyone else around you but automatically discount that there's any in you?"

"I—" She shook her head. "It's not that easy."

I began to protest, but she cut off the words with a shake of her head.

"I'll think about what you said, okay?" she whispered. "But . . . I've spent so long thinking I was protecting the world from this evil living inside me, just waiting to emerge. I can't just let that go after a couple of nice words in the dark."

"Why not?"

"Why? I—"

"Yes, why not?" I pressed. "I've seen you make split-second decisions on a mission plenty of times—even changing course mid-stride when things go awry," I added when it seemed like she was going to be the one protesting this time around. "You get new information, you assess, you move on."

"Dan."

"It's true, and you know it is."

Her expression hardened. "Enough. Stop pushing. You're not my father—"

"Thank God for that."

Now that expression turned hurt, and I realized what I'd implied. "Shit, Ava. I didn't mean it like that, like there's something wrong with you because there's clearly a whole multitude wrong with him." I mentally smacked myself. "You're different."

Silence.

Then, "How do you know?"

"I know it like I know without having to think exactly where you're going to be on a mission, that I don't have to worry about covering my back when you have it. I know you're different because you're devoted and strong and smart as hell, because you always carry a piece of candy in your pocket, just in case we come across a kid who's scared or sad or just deserves a piece of candy."

"Those are just little things."

I sighed and sat back. "Those are all the things, sweetheart."

"Don't—"

"Call you sweetheart?" I reached for her boot again, managed to free it from the most swollen part of her ankle. "I know. I'm sorry. I won't let it happen again."

"No." She hissed when I began working her sock down. "That's not what I was saying."

"Then what?"

"I don't mind it."

"Don't mind what?"

"The whole calling me sweetheart thing." A beat. "You used it at the cabin."

"Yes." I carefully set the insoles on either side of her ankle, noting that while it was definitely broken, it was not quite as bad as I had imagined.

"And—" She hesitated for a long moment then sighed. "Why is this so hard?"

"It's never easy to ask for what you truly want."

Brown eyes on mine. "Is that what this is?"

I froze, biting back a curse when she hissed as I began wrapping the shoelace, securing the insoles in place. "What you want?" I asked lightly. "Yeah. I hope so. Because I definitely don't want to be all alone in the want department."

"I—" She broke off, but not in pain. Her brows were furrowed. "I was going to say I've never been afraid to go for what I want. Except . . ."

"Except?"

"Except, I don't think I've ever considered *what* I really wanted. I've worked to make myself strong, to be able to protect myself. I worked to be a good agent, to do some good when my family has done so much evil." Ava sighed. "But I don't think I've ever actually stopped for a moment and considered what I was feeling in my heart."

"It was too scary," I murmured, securing the last of the lace around her ankle and sitting back.

"No," she said. "Well, yes, *that.* But also, it was easier to not feel, especially when the only thing I *could* feel was how broken I was inside. It was safer to not ever look deep into what I really wanted." She sat up with a wince. "I'm just not convinced that—"

She screwed up her face and cut off her words.

"Look, this isn't a conversation I'd ever have normally," she said. "Not even during that week with you. Yes, when we were together. Yes, a part of me reveled in feeling free and shared more with you than anyone ever. But in my head, there was always a natural conclusion to our interlude—us going back to being teammates, you finding someone worthy of you, me carrying on with what I did best. Working." She bit her lip. "Because I couldn't let anyone in. But . . . I guess a big part of me—has always wanted someone to be close to. I just don't know if I'll ever be the kind of person who can *actually* do that."

"You're telling me that the strongest woman I know is just going to give up?" She rolled her eyes toward the ceiling. "Because that's bullshit. You never give up on anything, least of all simply because you're scared."

"Ugh." A frown pulled her brows together. "You know you're annoying, right?"

"It's a gift." I slid close to her, took her hand. "But you know you're a woman I respect, one I care about, one I *like* a whole hell of a lot." I bit back anything more than that, knowing I was already in dangerous territory, that we'd already taken about five steps forward. "And even though you've done your best to keep me firmly away, completely locked out, you've made yourself at home in my heart anyway."

She inhaled sharply. "Dan."

"Too much?"

A shake of her head.

"Good." I lay down next to her, careful to not jostle her. "Now, tell me again why you think, for some insane reason, that vanilla ice cream is better than chocolate."

A blip of quiet before her mouth curved up. "Next, you'll be asking me to explain why the movie versions of books are better than the actual books."

"Blasphemy!"

"Okay," she said. "Then try to convince me otherwise."

So, as the sun began to descend in the sky, we stayed locked in that cell, talking about movies.

TWENTY

Southern Italy
Unknown hrs local time

Ava

THEY CAME for us when the sun's light had dimmed in that sliver, leaving us in the muted glow of approaching dusk.

We'd talked for a long time, moving on from the heavy stuff and back to the lighter topics that had filled our days in Georgia. But it wasn't all just old mission talk or pop culture. It was . . . *more.*

I'd told him more about Isa, how she used to always sneak me dessert—after my father had declared I was getting too fat and would be going without. I'd told him about how I'd loved putting just my toes in the ocean and hated getting my hair wet. Oh, we'd definitely argued about our opposing opinions of books versus movies, but it hadn't been the sole thing connecting us.

I'd shared.

And so had he.

He'd told me about Brit and how she was starting to think

about what her career might look like after her playing days were over. I'd told him how I'd hidden during those years after leaving this home, pawning jewelry I'd stolen, stretching cash until I'd made it over the border to Germany and had been able to find work. He'd told me about a recent visit to his parents.

It was give and take, allowing those walls down enough that he could creep in.

And . . . not being terrified.

Okay, only halfway terrified.

But a girl couldn't have everything, could I?

Case in point, I'd just rested my head on his shoulder—go baby steps!—when we heard them coming down the hall again.

This time, however, they took both of us.

"Come."

How? Frankly, it was a miracle I was standing. Already, the narrow space was spinning around me, my makeshift splinted ankle throbbing, making me waver as I attempted to balance on one foot.

Dan shifted behind me, taking a position at my back, covering my blind spot.

My heart. The organ I'd thought long frozen over, or maybe shattered into pieces that could never be reformed, swelled, filled with hope, with . . . feelings, okay? I was feeling *all* the feelings, after talking about *all* the things, after experiencing *all* the emotional events of the last hours and days.

Insanity.

But that was life.

Maybe it was the kissing. Maybe it had melted my brain in that elevator.

Or maybe . . . it was just inevitable.

As in, perhaps being in Dan's presence was enough to enact an inescapable erosion of my walls, not just because of the spark of desire between us, but because he was a *good* man. Because I respected him. Because he never looked at me like I was broken or wrong or evil.

Even after knowing all of the bad.

He just treated me like a normal woman, even after he'd found out I'd grown up among the Toscalos, after I'd told him about Isa.

Focus.

Right. I know I'd been spending all this time with my feelings and being all . . . well, human.

But now wasn't the time for Human Ava.

It was the time for Icy, Focused, Kickass Ava.

Lifting my chin, I faced the group of men in front of me. Three were familiar faces—my cousins—and the two I didn't recognize looked to have barely reached adulthood.

I took a halting step in the direction my cousin indicated, attempting to ignore the pain shooting up my leg and torso.

Movement at my back had me stiffening.

Then, "Me," Dan whispered, as he scooped me up into his arms.

One of the goons shifted as though he were going to stop Dan, but Dan just held me closer and said, "She's injured and won't make it far. Do you want us to go with you or not?"

Silence.

Then a brusque nod.

And I decided to play up the weak woman angle. Perhaps the fuckers would underestimate me. Maybe they would think me too hurt and wouldn't pay attention, and then we'd have our way out.

Of course, it wasn't hard to play up the weak woman angle.

Not when I was hurting and dizzy from blood loss and the pain.

"Focus, Ava," Dan hissed.

I nodded. "I am."

"Your—"

"No talking," one of the men snapped. He turned and started walking, leading us through the series of corridors I knew all too well. Down. Guiding us farther into the twisted maze of rocks. My father loved this castle on the hillside, loved the ancient hallways and tangled passageways, the small cells, the dark, damp space.

I'd played in these halls when I was a child, hiding and seeking and laughing like a lunatic anytime I was spotted by one of my father's men.

Until I'd realized that the halls led to cells.

Fun times.

Tearing my gaze from the walls, I glanced up at Dan. He held my gaze and tapped the inside of my elbow, where the tracker was implanted. I knew it was his way of reminding me that though we might feel like they were alone, KTS would have our backs. The tracking chips were another new technology, so at least there was a good chance they wouldn't be compromised, if it truly was the former KTS agent, Daniel, who was the one feeding information and working with KTS's enemies.

And we had a chip outside the heavy rock walls, so even if my signal was compromised, Dan's wouldn't be.

I covered his hand with my own, squeezed lightly.

Then I rested my head on his chest and pretended to be out of it.

Sadly, it was all too easy.

TWENTY-ONE

Southern Italy
Unknown hrs local time

Dan

MY RIBS THROBBED, my mind spun, and Ava in my arms
was all too right.

And we were being led deeper into some sick fucker's
dungeon.

A sick fuck whose household she'd grown up in.

I wanted to refuse on principle to follow them, refuse to go
anywhere near that room I'd been taken to before, refuse to
carry Ava down this fucking sicko path.

Her father, Frankie, was on the top of KTS's list of bad guys
to take down. He'd ruled southern Italy with an iron fist, single-
handedly driving out progress and better opportunities for the
people who live there by expanding his criminal enterprises. He
looped in young boys, got them running drugs and laundering
money. Families living there had to pay protection money from

their meager earnings, making it extremely difficult to move away, to find better and safer opportunities.

And Frankie used them as fodder.

Not giving a fuck if they were killed or injured, not giving a damn for the families left behind.

All while he lived in an expensive castle above the glittering Mediterranean Sea.

The Italian who'd ordered us to follow him stopped in front of a familiar large wooden door, knocking once on the thick board. A voice called from inside, and then the panel was pulled open.

And then we were face-to-face with Frankie Toscalo himself.

Ava's spine stiffened, tension invading every part of her body that was touching mine.

"*Bella*," Frankie said.

Ava shifted slightly in my arms, and I got the message, carefully setting her down, not liking the way her cheeks went even paler, nor the fragile way she held herself. But her voice was steady. "What do you want, Frankie?"

The man was plump and balding, the buttons of his white silk button-down slightly bulging, the remnants of his hair nearly white. He leaned against the wall across the room from us, arms casually overlapped, smile unaffected by the disdain in his daughter's voice.

"I'm your father, daughter."

"You stopped being that a long time ago," Ava spat.

He strolled toward us, goons at his back. "Ah, you wound me, *bella*." He stroked a hand down Ava's face then cupped her cheek. She jerked away and stumbled several paces away.

I stepped closer—or tried to anyway. Hands gripped my arms, wrenched me back.

"I cared for you. I provided food and love—"

She laughed darkly. "You never loved me."

I didn't expect him to move so fast.

One second he was standing a foot in front of Ava, his eyes darkening, and the next, he had burst forward and punched her in the stomach.

She crumpled to the floor, a cry of pain escaping.

I tore my arms free from my captor's grasp and jumped forward, moving between them, blocking her father when he would have kicked out at her, and earning a blow from the goons behind us for my trouble. I pushed Frankie back then spun, knocked one of the fuckers on his ass, reached out for another, but I couldn't do more than that because—

Click.

"Don't fuck with me." Soft, deadly words that nonetheless easily reached my ears.

And sent a cold chill down my spine.

I slowly rotated back.

Frankie didn't lower the gun from where it was pointed at Ava. "How did KTS know about the hotel?"

Silence. From both me and Ava.

A gunshot rang out.

I lunged forward again, trying and failing to put my body between her and the bullet.

But I couldn't outpace gunpowder or a piece of metal flying three times the speed of sound, and the sound it made sinking into Ava's flesh was fucking sickening.

Then I heard the *click* again.

"How?" he repeated.

Ava spat.

The gun never wavered, Frankie's finger tightening—

"We had a source," I said.

"Who?"

"He's dead."

Click.

A bullet exploded from the gun, hitting the stone floor next to her shoulder, sending chips of rocks flying up into the air.

I straightened from where I'd thrown my body over Ava. She'd gone quiet and deathly still, and panic was tearing through me. "You can put as many bullets as you want into me," I said. "Into your daughter, but that won't change the fact that the man is dead."

Silence.

Frankie stepped closer, pressed the gun to my temple. I could disarm him in an instant, but I held my ground, knowing the other men in the room had weapons that could be drawn before I could do anything to get us to safety. "Our source told us that something big was going to go down at the hotel on that date," I said. "We had no other information besides that."

Frankie's eyes were so much like Ava's.

A deep chocolate brown.

Except where Ava's had a warmth I could sense, even when there was ice on the surface, Frankie's were like looking into a black fucking hole. There was no soul inside, no caring.

He'd end us without a second thought the moment we weren't useful.

Silence filled the space, no one speaking, the only noise breaking the quiet Ava's rasped out breaths.

The sound both frightened and calmed me.

She was still breathing.

She was having a hard fucking time breathing.

Frankie kicked Ava's ankle, eliciting a sharp cry from her. "What is the name of—"

A rumbling shook the floor.

For a second, I thought it was an earthquake. I hadn't felt too many of those growing up on the East Coast, but I'd been through a handful while visiting my sister in California and several more on various deployments.

Frankie frowned, glanced at the door, the floor.

But unlike the earthquakes I'd be through, this one didn't go on, a wave of movement with a slowing end. This one stopped abruptly, the shaking cutting off.

Right before more rumbling began.

Only this time, closer and sharper.

And . . . I knew the cavalry was coming.

I launched myself forward, knocking Frankie to the ground. The older man dropped the gun and it clattered along the stones, out of reach of both of us. Shouts rang out, boots coming toward me, hands gripping my shirt, pummeling at my back, even as I fought to control the man beneath me.

Frankie was older and fatter than me *and* a hell of a lot meaner.

Or, at least, a much dirtier fighter.

Because I was feeling pretty fucking mean.

I took a blow to the back of my head that made my ears ring, my temple throb, black edge into my vision, and barely missed the fist Frankie threw up.

Another gunshot rang out, and the pressure on my back stopped.

I pinned Frankie in place with an elbow, risked a glance to my left, and saw that Ava was sitting up, the gun held in her hands. She had one eye shut, and I watched as she fired off another shot and took down another of the men.

Frankie bucked, nearly tossing me off, and I redoubled my efforts, applying firm pressure to his carotid as more shots rang out. Too many to be from one gun, but the rapid *pop-pop-pop* ended after a few more seconds, right around the same time that Ava's father finally slumped into unconsciousness.

I hopped up and ran over to Ava.

"I'm okay," she rasped. "Tie 'em up."

Nodding, I hauled ass, luckily stumbling onto a pile of cable ties on a table to make it easier to restrain the men. I could unfortunately surmise their purpose, and it was infuriating to think what Frankie had done already and had intended to do to his daughter in this room. But for the moment, I pushed the anger away and concentrated on restraining any of the men with a pulse, binding wrists and ankles with the cable ties.

Then I moved back to Ava, yanking at the tongue of my boot and pulling out the emergency bandage and clotting agent.

I lifted her shirt, assessed her wound.

Frankly, it wasn't a great assessment.

The location—in the middle of her abdomen—was shit and there wasn't an exit wound—which meant the bullet was still lodged in there and could be causing even more damage. Paired with the knife wound, the broken ankle . . .

Not. Good.

I tore the packet of clotting agent open with my teeth. "Ready?"

She inclined her head. "Go."

I poured on the powder, her hiss of pain singeing through me as it bubbled and began working on her skin. Working quickly, I wrapped the bandage around her torso, pushing firmly to keep the pressure in place then tying it off as tightly as I dared, all while trying to ignore the way a cry emerged from her throat, the yelp escaping from between her tightly pressed lips. But fuck, hearing that sliced me to the quick.

"Here," I said once I'd finished. I handed her two guns, shoved another two into the waistband of my pants, one in the front where she could reach easily, one in the back that would be more difficult for her but would allow me to grab it with a single hand as necessary. "Ready?"

She started to push up, and I bent, picking her up into my arms as carefully as possible.

More pained sounds. A grunt that was quickly stifled.

"I can walk," she said.

No, she couldn't. We both knew that, but I didn't waste time arguing. Instead, I held her closer. "You're the better shot," I reminded her. "And you know this place. Be my eyes and my guide. I'll be the brute strength." Forcing my lips up, I added, "You know that's all I'm good for anyway."

"Hard-headed?"

"Hard *something*."

She snorted then winced.

And I felt like an even bigger asshole.

"I wouldn't be so quick to be an avenging angel to that one," came a cold voice.

Frankie was awake. Great.

"She's a Toscalo through and through," he said. "And she enjoyed proving it when she turned on her friends, betrayed anyone who ever took care of her. Look at me. I was—"

Ava shot him between the eyes.

Blood bloomed on his forehead; his body collapsed back onto the floor.

Her brown eyes were ringed with pain when they met mine. "I'm *not* that."

I didn't bother wasting any grief for the man. Frankie was a fucking bastard, and the world was a better place without him. I just turned for the door.

Maybe that made me a bad person.

Maybe I should feel a blip of guilt or concern that she'd executed him without preamble.

But I'd seen too much of Frankie's deeds, knew too much of what would become his legacy to judge her for that. And I'd seen too many powerful, violent men hurt and manipulate and

torment everyone around them without ever paying the consequences to think anything but good riddance, this man was
gone.

Especially when her voice shook as she said, "I'm not him. I
never will be."

"No, you won't," I told her.

By then, I'd reached the door. I shifted her, reached for the
handle, and asked for a third time, "Ready?"

Her eyes slid closed then opened back up, the pain hidden,
determination written in every line of her face.

"Let's go."

TWENTY-TWO

Southern Italy
Unknown hrs local time

Ava

MY HEAD WAS GETTING FUZZY, pain was making my reflexes slow.

My vision was blurry unless I closed one eye, and if I did that, I couldn't very well be Dan's eyes if I was only using one, could I?

But I didn't have time to worry about it, not when I had to focus.

"Go to the end of the corridor and turn right."

A nod as he picked up the pace.

We made it out of the room without seeing any guards and began winding our way to the surface, so I was trying not to focus on how the jarring from Dan running sent bolts of agony shooting through me every step of the way. The rumbling was continuing, stopping and starting at regular intervals, and that gave me hope it was Laila and the rest of KTS coming to say them with guns blazing.

Because if it wasn't, if it was some other criminal organization attacking my father's compound and we suddenly needed to outrun two enemies, I knew we wouldn't make it.

I wouldn't make it.

I would slow Dan down.

As it was—

"Down!" I hissed.

Dan didn't hesitate, just dropped into a crouch.

I squinted, fired off two rounds, and one of my cousins hit the ground.

Family and blood and bullets and death. How many Toscalos would I be responsible for eliminating that day? And how many had been like me? Were innocent until they were pulled and coaxed and cajoled into a serious situation they couldn't get out of.

I'd managed to find a way to exit the family.

But it had taken years, and my survival after leaving the family had largely been due to me stumbling onto a KTS agent.

I'd helped Laila when she was injured, offering what little money I'd earned at my under-the-table waitressing job and letting Laila stay with me in my hidey hole until she'd been able to contact headquarters. Laila had brought me to KTS, offering protection. That protection had turned into self-defense training, and that training had transformed me into someone who was strong, who wouldn't be taken advantage of again.

And that training had brought alongside it a safe home and something that resembled a family.

Even though I had been so damned careful to keep Laila out.

My friend had gotten in anyway. Then Olive and Dan and Ryker.

"Clear," I murmured. "Take that right and then there should be a stairwell at the end. It leads upstairs."

We made it to the stairs and up the short flight.

And then we were creeping through a dimly lit room. It was large and open, the only barrier between the windows showing the sea in the distance a narrow stretch of wall separating the dining area from the rest of the space.

"I'm assuming you did me a favor, cousin?"

I stiffened at the sound of the voice. "Sergio," I murmured to Dan.

Footsteps on the marble floor, several men I didn't recognize coming out to flank my cousin, where he sat on a large cream couch.

One of them stepped close, whispered in his ear.

And I watched a sick smile spread on his lips.

"Are you the reason your dear father has a bullet in his skull?"

I swallowed, whispered. "Three exits. One back down in the dungeon, another through the kitchen via a servant's door, the final one behind that couch there."

Dan nodded slightly.

"I'm leaving," I said. "You do with the family what you want."

I'd take Sergio out with KTS's help another time.

Today, I wanted to get the fuck out of here alive.

Still in Dan's arms, still feeling very much like a pathetic damsel in distress, I held tight as Dan shifted, moved toward the door I'd indicated with my head."

"Not so fast," Sergio said casually. He glanced at his watch.

Clicks surrounded us. Safeties disengaged in unison.

Another rumbled shook the house. "Ah, right on time. Your pathetic little play army is trying to blast into the dungeons." A nod. "Go take care of that." Two men peeled off, pounding across the floor and slipping through the narrow door that led back into the dungeon. "Now," his cold gaze fixed me in place. "Where were you? Ah"—he tapped a finger to his chin—"you were about to tell me all that KTS knows about the family."

"I'm not telling you anything." I knew that much, even though my head was growing fuzzy.

Sergio lifted a gun from his lap. "I think I can convince you."

"I'm getting really tired of guns being pointed at us," I muttered.

"Now, cousin." Sergio casually lifted a shoulder. "Or I pull the trigger."

"Hang tight," Dan whispered.

He spun, and I held up my own gun, using the angle he gave me to get off several shots. But the poor light and the distance meant that I'd missed, Sergio diving to the side, firing rounds back at us, the rest of the goons following suit. Dan jumped behind a wall, hitting the deck just as more feet pounded into the room, as more bullets began to fill the air.

Attempting to breathe through the jarring impact as we hit the tile floor, I knew I wasn't going to last much longer.

Not in a fight for our lives.

I was a liability.

"Go," I said, gasping out a breath. "I'll cover you." I swallowed hard. "The servant's door is down the hall. Go out the kitchen and take the path down to the beach. Follow it, and you'll find the dock." I lifted my gun, returned fire. "There are always boats there. Take one and get the fuck out of here."

"Ava."

I snagged the gun from the waistband of his pants, blinked against the plaster bursting into shards from the bullets hitting our faces. "Hurry, Dan."

"I'm not leaving you."

Already my fingers were having a hard time squeezing the trigger.

"You need to go—"

He gripped my chin, pressed his mouth to mine roughly. "I'm *not* leaving you. So, get that the fuck out of your mind right now."

"You *have* to!" I returned fired. "Dan. I can't be the reason you don't make it out of here. Think about your family. Your sister—"

"Fuck that," he snapped, grabbing me and shifting us down the wall as more bullets pinged repeatedly against the plaster. He grabbed a table, threw it on its side, and shoved me behind it. "We're both getting out of here alive. So fucking suck it up, agent. Get your head out of your fucking ass and clear our path to that exit."

Someone peeked around the opening.

Dan fired, and the man went down.

"*Now,* Ava."

I scrambled to focus, to not keep arguing with the stubborn man. "We need to get across the opening behind us. From there, we'll have a clear shot to the exit through the servants' quarters. Right at the hall, a hundred meters down. The door is hidden behind a bookcase."

"Got it." He rose, grabbed a mirror from the wall. "Ready with a shot?"

Hobbling forward, following close behind him, I waited until we were in position, then hissed, "Go!"

He leaned around the wall and slid the mirror across the tile, sending it right toward my cousin and his men.

I leaned, too, then closed one eye, focused before firing off a shot, and . . . it shattered.

Glass burst into the air, blinding the men momentarily.

It was enough. Dan scooped me up and ran like the fucking

devil was behind us. And maybe it was. Because this house, this fucking house of horrors—

"Here," I said.

He skidded to a stop, shoved the bookcase open, then we slipped inside and came face to face with—

His gun was out in an instant.

"Wait," I said, recognizing the woman, pushing Dan's arm down. "I know her. She's—"

"Eva?" she whispered.

My eyes drifted to her arm, to the arm, the hand that was no longer there. "Isa."

She stepped forward, touched my cheek with the other hand, and it was just like when I was a child, when she'd wipe my tears away. "You're hurt, *caro*."

"Yes, I—"

Voices echoed through the hall.

We all looked to the door.

"Go." Isa spoke in rapid Italian. "Hurry. Through the garden. My car is parked behind the vines. Keys are under the seat." She reached up and threw a lock that was installed on the inside of the door, just before it started rattling, men yelling through the wood. "Leave and don't ever come back to this place."

"Isa, I'm so sorry," I said. "I didn't think about—"

"This is not the time for that," Isa said. "You need to leave."

"I didn't mean to—"

Warm fingers over mine. "I know, *caro*," she murmured. "I forgive you. I've always forgiven you. And as much as I want you to tell me all about your life these last years, you need to go."

"Come with us," Dan said.

"No," Isa said. "I can't. Now *go*, Eva."

"Isa," I whispered.

Fingers on my cheek. "I know," she said softly. "Now go. Do good. Be happy."

Dan waited for her to step back. "You sure you won't come."

Isa nodded.

And he didn't ask again, didn't wait any longer, just hustled down the stairs, following my whispered instructions. And it was getting harder and harder for me to even whisper them. Blood dripped down my side, soaked into my pants. My ankle hurt more with every bump, until it threatened to swallow me whole.

I dropped one of the guns, unable to hold onto it any longer, focused on holding tightly to the other, on trying to remember how many shots there were left in it.

There couldn't be many, not after the twisting halls and the shooting in the family room.

Was it three?

Maybe two?

"Which way?"

I blinked, realized we'd emerged into a kitchen. "Straight out. Brick fence. Right. Follow it until the gate."

We were out into the sunshine a few seconds later, sprinting through the trees, and then I found myself on the ground, surrounded by a cluster of comically cheerful wildflowers.

Dan backed up and threw his shoulder at the wooden gate.

It groaned but didn't give way.

Not for three more painful, jarring hits.

Then it burst outward, and I was in his arms again, and we were running.

A yell sounded behind us, more gunshots, and I knew we weren't going to make it.

There were too many of them. I was slowing him down.

We would never make it to the car, and even if we somehow did, we wouldn't make it out of the compound.

Dan just needed to leave me. This wasn't some martyr bull-shit. I didn't want to stay here, but fuck, I also couldn't be the reason he didn't make it out alive.

I opened my mouth, started to speak. "You need to—"

And the world exploded around us.

TWENTY-THREE

Southern Italy
Unknown hrs local time

Dan

IT WAS TOO FUCKING early in the evening for bloodshed.

But evil didn't always wait for a convenient hour.

"You need to—"

Ava didn't get to finish her order for me to leave her—not that I would have done it—because an explosion rent the air.

I dove toward the wall, trying to take the brunt of the fall, before rolling us and protecting her body with mine. My ears rang, cuts littered my bare skin, and I knew the constant jarring couldn't possibly be good for her injuries.

When the noise stopped, I started to lift her into my arms.

But then my nape prickled. I released her, spun with my gun extended, and . . .

Breathed a long sigh of relief.

"Fucking hell," I said, staring at Ryker and Laila. "Took you guys long enough."

"Maybe next time don't leave your tracker someplace you're not."

We didn't have enough time to get into the details, so I simply turned back to Ava, saw she was on her feet, gun in hand, balance teetering.

Her chin came up, and she hobbled forward. "Let's go."

And then she collapsed.

I was already moving, caught her before she hit the ground. "Let's go," I said, repeating her sentiment.

Laila nodded. "Car's this way."

The car turned out to be an armored vehicle, the engine idling, with Olive behind the wheel. When she saw us coming, she got out, helped me get Ava into the backseat. Doors slammed, Ryker started driving, and Laila got on her phone, calling into headquarters.

But I wasn't paying attention to that.

My gaze was on Ava.

On Olive and her somber expression.

On the growing pile of blood-soaked bandages filling the floor of the vehicle as we drove.

Ava was so, so pale.

There was so much blood on her skin, on the seat, on her clothing, on the dressings.

And clearly not enough *in* her.

THE DAYS that followed were some of the worst of my life.

Ava was a woman who could go very still, waiting for hours to get the perfect shot. But even when she was motionless, there was still so much life in her, prickling beneath the surface.

Now . . . she was quiet.

No spark.

No life.

Just a slender, pale woman hooked up to too many machines.

And she slept on. Never rising from unconsciousness as the hours passed—not as Ryker drove like the hounds of hell were behind us as Laila directed him to a KTS safe clinic, not as Ava was stabilized and wheeled aboard a KTS plane, not as she arrived at KTS headquarters and was brought directly to the clinic where Olive watched over her until Laila had pulled the doctor away.

Olive had been dead on her feet, nearly unconscious herself as she watched every monitor, checked every stitch and bandage, ran herself ragged with every change in blood pressure and pulse.

It wasn't until Laila pointed out that her fatigue might risk Ava's recovery that Olive had finally left the room.

And I had stayed.

Maybe from the outside nothing between me and Ava had changed.

We were still teammates, still agents who sometimes put our lives on the line, who were occasionally seriously injured in the line of fire.

Maybe people would think a handful of kisses and some conversations didn't change anything.

But it was more than just kisses and words.

It was whispered memories in a dark cell, a bond forming when shit got scary. It was her being so willing to sacrifice herself when she'd kicked ass to get me out of the warehouse safely several weeks before. It was pain in her clear brown eyes after she'd taken the shot to kill her father. It was a sliver of light in a claustrophobic space, a glimpse of a life that hadn't broken her but would have shattered so many other people before.

It was her limping forward with a broken ankle and a stab wound in her side.

It was . . . Ava.

I'd seen inside the carefully built walls, and I had so much fucking respect for the woman.

But she was still and silent . . . and it killed me to see her like that.

A soft knock on the door had me glancing up, and it spoke to how tired *I* was that I hadn't heard it open.

Laila stood on the threshold and took one look at me before pointing down the hall. "Shut-eye. Now."

"Lai—"

"That's wasn't a suggestion," she said.

"You're giving me orders now?" I asked.

Technically, she was the team leader, of course, but it wasn't a common thing for her to outright tell us to do something. Usually, we worked within loose parameters Laila laid out, discussed and came up with a plan of action together. She didn't order us around . . . unless we were at risk of hurting someone or . . . ourselves.

"Dan," she said. "You're of no use to her right now. Your reflexes are slow. Your senses dulled." She shrugged, her tone no-nonsense and not the least bit soft. "You couldn't protect her from a fly. You're dead on your fucking feet. You need to sleep."

Pissed off, I straightened, shoved down the fatigue. "I'm fine."

"Definitely not fine," she said. "Which is why I'm advising you to go the fuck to sleep so that when she wakes up, you're ready to be there for her."

"More orders," I muttered.

Laila rolled her eyes. "Look, we both know the only reason you're not running your own team is because of Ava. You've been in love with her for years, and you decided to stay on my team because it's the only way you can be close to her."

"I—"

She sighed, pushed off the wall. "Look. I've been there," she reminded me. "On *both* sides—too fucking scared to go after the person I wanted and spending every waking moment longing for the single individual who I thought might fit me perfectly."

"Laila—"

Laila gripped my arms, shook me lightly. "She's strong. You know that." A sigh. "But sometimes those that seem the strongest on the outside are the ones who need the most care on the inside."

"You know, I would do that for her in an instant," I said. "She's—"

"Your everything," Laila finished for me when I faltered. "I get that. Like I said, I've been there." She stepped back, crossed her arms. "But D, I honestly don't know if she's ready for you or a relationship or to let *anyone* in. She's been so hurt and closed down for a very long time. I've known her for nine years, and while I've seen glimmers of the woman she is beneath those shields, and I consider her a close friend, *and* I would *never* hesitate to have her at my back on a mission . . ." She sighed. "I'm . . . just not sure if she's ready to let another person near her heart."

"She *is* ready to let someone in," I protested. "We—"

Laila shook her head. "You can't know that."

In all honesty, I wanted to argue, to tell her about the connection, the week in Georgia, the conversations in the cell. I wanted to tell her about the look in Ava's eyes outside the compound, the way she'd pushed me to leave her, and the relief in them when I hadn't. I wanted to tell Laila about the pain on Ava's face after she'd taken the shot that killed her father and how she'd let me hold her hand in the dark cell, allowing me in past those walls, just the smallest bit.

I wanted to tell Laila about Ava's determination.

To not let her father break her. To stay strong even though the odds were against us. To make whatever sacrifices were needed in order to get me out.

Of course, I'd rather Ava be that determined to get herself out, but I was just as stubborn, could go toe-to-toe with her when it came to her safety. I'd make any necessary sacrifices to help her in any way.

Because we were more than teammates.

She'd let me in, and I wasn't going to allow her to wall me back out.

That was what made me certain that the bond we'd formed was permanent.

I was in. Because *she'd* let me in.

And I wasn't going backward.

"I *know* it," I said. "I know we've crossed the first hurdle. She cracked open the door, and I'm *in*."

There was doubt written across her face. "Dan," Laila said on a sigh. "I don't know that you can honestly get into someone who's done everything to keep everyone out." Her lips pressed flat. "If she doesn't want someone in, it doesn't matter how persistent or stubborn you are, you aren't getting in. She'll rebuild those walls, and they'll be a hundred times stronger."

"It's not like that."

A nod. An expression that told me Laila was unsure, even in the face of my determination and stubbornness. "Sleep, Plantain. Everything else will hold till you've had shut-eye."

More arguments on the tip of my tongue.

More arguments I knew wouldn't change Laila's mind, nor what would happen between me and Ava.

More arguments I swallowed, pushed down, ignored for the moment.

Because Laila was right.

Ava might have let me in, might have allowed me to see a part of her that the rest of the world wasn't privy to, but it wasn't like she wasn't going to keep the walls down, the castle gate flung wide. She would retreat.

I just needed to make sure she didn't retreat from me.

Which meant I needed to be conscious and well-rested if I had a hope in hell of winning the battle that lay ahead.

TWENTY-FOUR

Northeast England
KTS Headquarters
19:47hrs local time

Ava

THE FIRST THING I was aware of was the noise.

A steady *beep-beep, beep-beep, beep-beep.* The *woosh* of a fan. Quiet footsteps as water turned off then back on.

"You should go sleep again," came a soft female voice. I swam through the fog, tried to place it. Everything was soft and fuzzy and heavy and slow.

"Not yet."

"*Dan.*"

"I'll rest soon," he said. "I promise."

Dan.

Dan.

The memories poured back into my brain, as quickly as the bullets had flown in that compound, as quickly as our tide had turned at the hotel—

The shipment.

Kids. Women. Men.

"I'm worried about you," Olive—yes, the fog had cleared enough that I recognized Olive's voice. "You're hardly eating or sleeping. You need to rest soon, or I'll pull rank."

"A few more hours then I'll rest."

"I'm holding you to that."

"Roger, Dr. Evil."

A sigh. "Shut it, you." Footsteps moving away. "I'll see you in two hours."

The door opened and closed with a soft *click*.

Warm fingers covered mine. "I know you're awake."

My eyes flew open.

I was in a clinic, and though the initial glance didn't tell me where in the world I was, it was enough for me to grasp that we were in one of KTS's buildings.

"Headquarters," Dan said, and my gaze flicked to his. "It was touch and go there for a bit, so Olive flew you back here."

"*That's* why I feel like I got hit by a truck?"

"A gunshot, a broken ankle, and a knife wound will do that to a girl." His fingers convulsed lightly in mine. "You in a lot of pain? Need me to go get Olive?"

"No," I said. "No more pain medicine. I need my head to be clear."

Already, tendrils of pain were threatening to pull me back under, but I needed to know. "Ryker and Laila? Are they okay?"

"The team is fine. No one was injured aside from you."

"Your head," I said, trying to lift my free arm to point at the fading purples and yellows on his temple and cheek. "Your ribs."

"Only a mild concussion and bruises."

"What about the shipment?"

His face clouded.

Fuck.

"The teams were in position, but nothing showed." He sighed. "The other two teams stayed after Laila realized we weren't responding to our coms. But they must have called it off. The ships you spotted from the room disappeared, and we weren't able to have air support in time to track them."

My brows drew down. "But why?"

His eyes met mine. "They were relocated."

"Daniel?" I asked, stomach sinking.

"Either that or there's someone else."

"Fuck."

A smile. "Yes," he said then reached up as though he were going to touch my cheek. But then he hesitated. "Okay?"

The *beep-beep, beep-beep, beep-beep* on the monitors sped up, betraying the twin feelings coursing through me: panic—would what we'd found in that dark hole still be there, and hope —it *had* to still be there, right?

Right?

I released a slow breath and nodded.

Dan's fingers brushed my cheek.

And . . . it was still there.

Warmth filling me at his touch, sparking through my veins, filling my heart with bubbling champagne.

Right before reality set in.

Because really?

Was it possible that the two of us might work out? Or was it more likely the affection in his eyes would fizzle out, that he would find something broken inside me, see the missing parts, and just . . . walk away?

"Release the lines," he whispered, fingers shifting to rub lightly between my brows. "It's just you and me and nothing else, okay?"

I made a face. "It's not that easy."

"Want me to turn out the lights?"

I giggled. Me. I actually giggled, a light tinkling laugh that I never in a million years would have expected to escape from my lips.

And the effect it had on Dan's face was incredible.

"God, I love it when you laugh," he murmured, almost reverently.

Which was more insanity.

Because I was just me. Just Ava, and I hadn't done anything that would have anyone looking at me like I'd hung the moon or speak to me like I was important. I was a tool, a pawn, an agent who put my body on the line.

Except . . . not anymore.

I wasn't the little girl who saw the bad in her family and wanted to be like them.

I wasn't the hurting teenager who finally understood the cost of doing that.

And I wasn't the terrified woman whose barbed exterior kept everyone at a distance for fear of being looked at too closely and being found lacking.

Better to be found lacking initially.

Or perhaps better yet to not be found at all.

"You found me," I whispered, not realizing at first that I'd spoken aloud, continuing the conversation in my head until Dan's hand shifted and cupped my cheek.

"I did," he said gently. "And I'm not letting you go."

Somehow, the words didn't terrify me.

Instead, they filled me with even more warmth. But I was still me. I was still Ava and just because I was maybe coming to the conclusion that I wasn't so broken or lacking or messed up, I was still me. Sharp and tough and with plenty of attitude.

"I don't need you to let go," I said. "I can free myself if I want to."

Unfortunately, the statement was punctuated with a yawn, my body reminding me that it had been through a huge trauma and I was lucky to be alive.

"True," Dan said. "But I'm good at taking a beating. So bring it on, sweetheart."

"Not, sweetheart," I argued on another yawn.

"Right." He shifted like he was going to stand. "I'll let you sleep."

"Dan?" I asked.

Gentle eyes on mine. "Yeah."

"Will you turn out the lights?"

Because dark suddenly wasn't so scary, because being stuck in a small, dimly lit space wasn't terrifying.

Because of Dan.

He understood what I was saying and nodded before standing up and walking to the door.

The lights flicked off.

TWENTY-FIVE

Northeast England
KTS Headquarters
20:01 hrs local time

Dan

"WHAT ARE YOU DOING?" she exclaimed as I reached the small chair that had become my bed over the last four nights.

I'd just turned off the lights, was getting ready to settle in and watch her sleep—until Olive kicked me out, that was—when Ava's sharp question reached my ears.

"Letting you sleep," I said.

"And"—I heard a *click*, saw the tiny spotlight over her bed turn on—"where are you planning on sleeping?"

I pointed at the chair.

She scowled. "That's tiny."

"It's a chair," I said. "What size do you expect it to be?"

"You can't sleep there."

I lifted a brow. Her scowl grew darker. "I believe that technically I'm the one who decides where I can sleep."

"This is my room," she pointed out.

"Is it?" I said, sitting down and letting my legs spread out in front of me.

"Dan."

"Hmm?" I asked, my eyes closing.

"*Dan.*"

"Hmm?" I asked again.

"You need to go to your room."

"I will," I told her. "When you do."

She glowered. "Why are you giving me shit when I'm recovering from a gunshot wound, a knife wound, and a broken ankle?"

I grinned. "Because I like you, sweet cheeks."

"Are you trying to piss me off?"

"Is it working?"

An annoyed sound and I half-expected her to order me to leave. Not that I would. Now that she'd woken up, I wasn't going anywhere.

"No," she snapped. "Stop grinning."

I couldn't help it. I burst out laughing . . . at least until I got beaned by a pillow.

"You're not funny," she declared.

"I know," I said. "But I like fighting with you."

"Ugh." She shifted in the bed, and I snatched up the pillow, hurrying over to her when it looked like she was going to attempt to get up. There were all sorts of monitors and tubes still attached to her, and I wasn't about to mess any of that up. As much as I was arguing, I'd leave before I'd risk her hurting herself.

I would go . . . then just sneak back later.

But when I reached the bed, it wasn't to find her attempting an escape. Instead, she slid to one side and lifted the edge of the blanket. "Come on then."

I froze, the pillow in my hands. "What?"

"Get your ass in this bed, so we can both get some sleep."

"I shouldn't—"

"You trying to pick a fight?" she asked. "Or are you getting in?"

I tucked the pillow behind her head. "I don't want to hurt you, sweetheart."

"You're hurting me by not letting me get some sleep," she pointed out, not inaccurately.

"You'll tell me if I hurt you?"

Those brown eyes rolled. "You won't hurt me, Dan."

The way she said that, with complete and utter conviction, stole my breath, made my heart squeeze tight. Because she believed it. And it was probably the only thing she could have said to make me climb into bed with her.

Which was an oxymoron, wasn't it?

Any other time I'd be diving between those sheets.

Tonight, however, I slid in carefully, slipping an arm beneath her shoulders, and holding my breath for a moment when she cuddled into me.

At least until she whispered, "Breathe, Dan."

Then I closed my eyes, relaxed, and breathed, just like she'd ordered.

19:14HRS

Two DAYS after Ava had woken up, Olive gave her the all-clear to leave the infirmary.

She was weeks—okay, *months* away from active duty— mostly due to her ankle, but also due to the wounds. After she'd gotten the blood loss under control and given Ava several trans-fusions to replace the blood she'd lost, Olive had needed to pump some serious antibiotics into Ava's system. And that was on top of an emergency surgery Ava had needed at the satellite base in order for Olive to remove the bullet.

Once Ava had been stable enough for transport, the whole team had flown back to England, to the better medical equipment, knowing that Ava would need the newest tech they had for physical therapy.

Save the life in the field.

Stabilize at the satellite base.

And then full recovery came at headquarters.

"I fucking hate this," she muttered as I wheeled her down the hall.

If she didn't have the broken ankle, she might have been able to make it by simply walking—albeit slowly—to her room. But with her ankle casted and the twin healing wounds on her abdomen, Ava wasn't in any position to be walking anywhere.

"Bitching won't change anything," I said.

A beat, her head tilting up to glare at me. "You were nicer in the cell."

"So were you."

She snorted, shaking her head when she saw my lips twitching. "Thanks for wheeling me," she muttered after a few minutes of rolling. "Olive and Laila threatened to put bells on the chair if I went by myself."

"Should I grab some cans from the kitchen and tie them to the wheels?"

"Like one of those *Just Married* cars?"

"Exactly."

"When I get her, I'll introduce Luna 2.0 to you"—another glare—"and your junk."

I winced. "No cans. Got it."

She didn't reply, but I watched her stifle a yawn and sink back a little more in the chair. As much as she hated the fact it was going to take her time to recover—she was right up there with my patience—that was just a fact.

"Stupid ankle," she muttered, something I'd heard already more than a few times. "Without it, I'd be back in a few weeks."

"Gotta get more graceful."

More glares.

"God, you're pretty." Her lips parted, face softening for a few moments. Then her eyes started to narrow again, and I added, "I'm still well-aware that you can kick my ass."

A nod. A pleased expression before she faced forward again.

I wheeled her to her room and opened the door.

"Dan," she breathed.

"What?" I asked, knowing full well what had given her that reaction. I'd arranged for a surprise, had snuck it into her room, wanting to keep working at those walls, wanting her to know I hadn't forgotten all of what had transpired in that cell.

She reached back and covered my hand, squeezing lightly.

I'd put some battery-operated candles on the small table that was in each of these rooms. A single chair, same standard issue, had been pushed to the side to give a full view of the rifle.

Matte black metal, sleek and sexy, and a perfect fit for this woman.

Luna 2.0 had arrived.

I pushed her to the table. "How did you—?" She broke off, shook her head.

"When Laila told you that Luna hadn't been recovered, I talked to Fred. He helped me get the newest model, but," I added, "he modified it so you'd have the scope and trigger you prefer."

Silence.

Absolute silence for an interminable moment.

Then her shoulders shook, and she sniffed.

Shit.

I dropped the handles and rounded the wheelchair, kneeling in front of her. "Shit, Ava. I'm sorry. I shouldn't—"

Fingers dropping to my lips, she shook her head, and when her gaze came to mine, I saw that her eyes were damp. "Thank you," she whispered. "This is the most thoughtful gift anyone has ever gotten me."

I kissed her palm, peeled her fingers free. "Weapons as a good gift. Check."

She snorted. "Wheel me closer, Jeeves. I've got to check out the goods."

Rising, I rolled her closer to the table, giving her a few minutes to get acquainted with her new best friend, and heading to the door when the soft knock came. Olive stood on the other side, eyes narrowed.

"No hanky-panky," she ordered, holding up a tray of food.

"Not on my radar," I said, which was a lie, of course. I would always want this woman, but also, she was recovering from her injuries. I could wait.

Narrowed blue eyes. "Lie." She patted my cheek. "But also, you're a good man. Feed the woman, let her become acquainted with her new best friend, and make sure you both get some sleep—those ribs are still healing."

"What's with women always giving me orders?" I mock-grumbled.

Another pat. "You're used to it." She said her goodbye, and I shut the door, turning back to see that Ava was on her feet—or rather *one* foot, sighting the scope.

"Seriously?" I asked, moving toward her, setting the tray on the table, and scooping her into my arms. "No weight on that foot, remember?"

"To the bed, minion," she said, pointing to the mattress. "I'm not going to argue with you if it infringes on my Luna time." Since I wanted her resting, I didn't return with any snark, just pulled back the covers, set her carefully on the bed, and propped her foot with a pillow. "Dan?"

"Hmm?" I said, moving back to the table and the tray of food.

My inner caveman was piqued, a chant of *food, rest, sleep, food, rest, sleep* on repeat in my brain.

"*Dan.*"

She snagged my hand, and I turned back.

A tug brought me closer.

Another tug even closer.

One more until our lips were a hairsbreadth apart.

And then she kissed me, slow and sweet and coaxing, but with so much heat that my knees actually shook by the time we pulled away.

"Thank you," she murmured against my mouth, and the love I felt for this woman was all-consuming and overwhelming and really fucking incredible.

I cupped her cheek, pressed one more light kiss to her lips.

And then I gave into my inner caveman.

Food. Relaxing. Sleep.

The sleep was my favorite part.

Because I got to hold her in my arms again.

TWENTY-SIX

Northeast England
KTS Headquarters
18:26hrs local time

Ava

A WEEK LATER, there was a knock on my door.

I was sitting up, staring at the report the tech team had sent over, and trying to figure out our next steps.

We'd run some remote surveillance on the other drops we'd managed to deduce from the initial files, but no trafficking had taken place on any of them. So, it had become clear that the Toscalos and Mikhailovas had changed tactics.

Whether they'd simply stopped trading in people for the moment or just changed the trade routes was still a question we needed answered.

"Come in," I called since it wasn't like I was fully mobile.

By the time I made it to the door at "Grandma Speed"—thanks to Laila for that one—the person on the other side would be turning gray.

The knob rotated, and the wooden panel opened.

I'd be lying if I said I wasn't disappointed that it wasn't Dan.

"Oh," Laila grumbled. "Don't look like that. Dan and Ryker are coming and bringing pizzas."

I frowned. "What are you talking about?"

"It's been a fucked-up couple of weeks. We're hanging out. We're eating pizza"—she pointed a finger at me—"and we're going to enjoy spending time as a team."

Another knock at the door before I could say anything.

Olive poked her head in, carrying a plate of what looked like brownies. She glanced at me working and frowned. "You're supposed to be resting. You won't get any treats if you're not resting."

I nodded to my foot, encased in the cast and elevated on a spare chair Dan had brought to my room for just this purpose. "I'm resting."

"I hope so," she said, pulling a bag out of her jacket pocket. "Otherwise, no cinnamon rolls for you."

She wafted the bag under my nose and immediately my stomach rumbled.

"Freshly baked?" I asked, able to feel the heat from the bag.

"Yup." A beat. "So, you working?"

I flicked a finger, made the laptop's screen go black. "Nope."

She handed over the bag.

"How'd you know?" I asked, opening the top and scooping out a fingerful of frosting.

"About your cinnamon roll addiction?" Olive shrugged when I nodded. "Same way I know you don't like chocolate and that for some inane reason, Ryker doesn't drink coffee—"

"Can't mess up this perfect temple," Ryker said as he pushed through the door, pizza box in hand.

"Says the man carrying a pizza with at least five types of meat on it," Dan said dryly. His eyes met mine, and I felt my heart pick up its pace. He'd slept in my bed every night for the last week. He'd helped me to the bathroom, washed my hair over the sink. He'd brought me coffee—because I sure as shit drank it—and he'd . . . been there, even when I'd been cranky.

And I had to face it; I'd been cranky a lot.

I wasn't used to not being busy.

Even between missions I was always training—either hand-to-hand combat training or working out in the gym or practicing at the range or even just prepping for the next mission. So to have had a week off, and five to seven more in my future, I was going a little stir crazy.

And maybe part of me was still half-expecting that Dan would get tired of my bullshit and back off, if he saw how much of a bitch I could be.

Instead, he just grinned.

Which usually resulted in me threatening to use Luna 2.0 on him.

And *that* resulted in him kissing me until I forgot to be grumpy.

I couldn't lie and say it didn't work.

Now, he and Ryker set the pizzas down, shoved my laptop onto a shelf, and moved me so they could drag the table to the foot of the bed.

"Hi," Dan murmured, pressing a kiss to the side of my neck as he deposited me near the headboard. Olive shoved a pillow under my cast, and Laila set a plate of pizza in my lap with a wink.

"Don't think I didn't see that," she whispered.

"No comments allowed from the team leader married to her underling," I muttered.

"Comments withheld." A beat. "But I'm happy to see you . . . well, happy."

"Exactly," Olive said, bouncing onto the bed next to me. "I

don't care who you're doing the nasty with"—she arrowed a glance at Dan—"and that's a metaphorical nasty, since she's not cleared for bedroom activities yet." That glare swiveled to me. "Well, technically you're not cleared for *any* activities yet."

"How about sniper practice?" I asked innocently.

"So much sass," she grumbled. "You always used to be so quiet and following my orders. You were my best patient."

"I was just your sneakiest," I told her. "Unlike those two, who complain every time and make it obvious."

"Hey!" Ryker said.

"Hey!" Olive said.

"Cat's out of the bag," Laila said. "You would have done better to hold that one to your chest."

I picked up a slice of pizza. "I just spent two days getting shot and stabbed and having bones broken. I killed my father—which I should probably feel guilty about, but I don't, so you tell me what kind of person that makes me—and then I confronted being back in a cell where I spent the better part of two years, one that gave me nightmares up until all the shooting and stabbing and bone-breaking. I think I'm done holding things to my chest."

Silence.

Then Dan sank down on the bed next to me, took my hand. "Two years?"

"Yup," I said then added dryly, "Anyone want to join me for the Toscalo family reunion?"

"If it means I get to obliterate them all, then yes," Ryker said.

"Agree," Laila said.

"I'm in," Olive said.

"You don't even have to ask," Dan said.

Aw.

Planning the destruction of my biological relatives. Good times.

"I think we'd better start with pizza," I said.

"Fair," Laila said, loading her own plate, "but if we get a chance to take out the Toscalos, we're going to take it."

"Agreed," Dan said.

I nodded.

Olive patted my hand.

Ryker met my eyes, inclined his head.

"In the meantime," Laila said. "We focus on the Mikhailova. And we focus on finding out whether the traitor in our midst is Daniel or someone else." Her brows furrowed, her expression intent and dead set. Then she relaxed, met my eyes, and smiled. "But first, pizza, and dishing on your and Dan's kissy-face activities."

"A lethal secret agent should not be saying words like *kissy-face*," Dan muttered.

"Don't try and put me in a box!" Laila exclaimed.

I sighed.

Olive grinned over at me. "Yes. We are women, hear us roar. Heels and guns, pizza and . . . all the kissy-facing."

I groaned.

Ryker burst out laughing.

"Remind me again why I let you guys into my room again?"

"We brought treats," Olive reminded her, snatching the paper bag with the cinnamon rolls back. "Anymore sass out of you, and I'll eat this myself."

"Tyrant," I muttered.

"Friend," she whispered as Laila grabbed the TV remote and she and Ryker began arguing over what movie to put on. "One who's glad to finally be able to see the real you." Olive leaned close. "And if you're wondering why you don't feel guilty about your father, it's because you're a good person, one who's had to make a lifetime's worth of tough decisions, and this one wasn't any different. You did what you had to do, and you're not going to look back and analyze every eyelash twitch."

I released a breath, touched to the core. All these years I'd done my level best to keep everyone out, and . . . I hadn't succeeded in the least. They knew me with or without the walls.

Then she gave me the death knell. The one that made my eyes sting. "And you're not going to feel guilty because we won't let you. We love you, Ava."

"Fuck," I muttered.

"What?" She frowned, even as Dan, all too familiar with my outbursts by now to react, simply squeezed my hand.

"I don't know how you assholes made a place in my heart," I told her. "But I'm damned glad you managed."

"Don't be too happy," Dan said. He jutted his chin toward Laila.

Who had just come to an agreement with Ryker about which movie to watch.

It was Christmas-themed. It was a Christmas-themed romantic movie.

In the middle of summer. In a room of secret agents.

I gestured to Dan to come close, leaned down to whisper in his ear. "Spoiler alert," I breathed. "I like it when the guy and the girl get their happy ending."

"I heard that!" Laila crowed.

"Good," I said.

And I decided that if this was the result of my walls falling, of me failing to keep everyone at a distance—a brightly lit room full of friends and a man I cared about deeply—then I could deal.

I grabbed Dan's shoulders and hauled him close.

Then I kissed him until my head spun.

Yeah, I could deal with that, too.

TWENTY-SEVEN

Central Georgia
Dan's cabin
18:36hrs local time

Dan

"HOW DID I let you convince me to deal with this humidity again?" Ava muttered, sitting up on the blanket I'd spread out for her. She poked a finger under the calf-high cast and began scratching. "This is going to smell like death when we get back to headquarters."

"A little sweat never hurt anyone," I said.

"Says you," she said, still grumbling. "I'm the one who's melting over here."

"Come melt over here," I said, still prone on the blanket, my head pleasantly full after the trio of whiskey-lemonades we'd drunk.

The sun was finally descending, taking the worst of the heat out of the air.

But the humidity was still intense, making our skin sticky, even in the shade of the trees.

"Fine," she said, rolling toward me. "But it's at your own peril."

Two weeks from that night in Ava's room, a little more than three since her injury, and she was finally more mobile. Her stitches were out, her antibiotics finished, and her cast had been cut down, replaced with a waterproof version fresh from Fred and his team.

She was hobbling around.

And going nuts being confined at headquarters.

So, when I'd floated the idea of spending a week here at the cabin, under the guise of me needing to check on the property—even though I'd had to pay for a vacation for my caretaker to get the place to ourselves—I'd hedged my bets.

She'd accepted without hesitation.

Thus, my plan to get her alone was successful.

"Too bad the peaches are all harvested," she murmured.

"Yeah," I said. "It was an early season."

"How'd you become a peach farmer?"

"Stupidly," I told her.

She laughed, pressed her body along my side. "Tell me."

"I was driving by after a mission, saw the *For Sale* sign, and figured I was nearing thirty and it was time to buy some property." I shrugged. "The trees were pretty. The house was decent. So, I put in an offer." A roll of my eyes. "I had no clue how in over my head I was. I'm hardly ever stateside, and now I owned a farm? Ridiculous."

"How long ago was that?"

"Six years."

"Well, the trees look to have survived."

"Thanks to Hank."

She propped her elbows on my chest. "Who's Hank?"

"The caretaker I hired about two weeks after realizing the actual size of this place."

"Smart."

I shook my head. "Necessary after a stupid purchase."

She brushed a kiss to my cheek. "Probably," she agreed. "But I am fond of this place." A smile. "I would like to experience it when it isn't a thousand degrees."

"Just a little hyperbole there."

"Shut it, you," she said.

"It's shut," I countered.

We lay in silence for a few minutes, the temperature lowering to something less in the vicinity of Seventh Circle of Hell and more to actually comfortable. But then Ava shifted and stretched back onto the blanket, her arms above her head.

My eyes drifted to her breasts, mouth watering.

We'd done very little *kissy-facing* as Laila called it, mostly because the team had been hanging out together and because I'd been forcing myself to not pounce on her like the starving beast I felt like.

I fucking loved her body.

But she'd been injured.

Was still healing.

So, though I'd held her every night since she'd woken in the infirmary, I hadn't allowed my brain to even consider anything more than that and the occasional kiss.

She moaned softly, and my eyes caught on the shimmering skin at the base of her throat, the way her lips, plump and tempting, parted as she breathed slowly and steadily. How her breasts lifted and fell in time to her breathing, the slightest jiggle visible in the V of her T-shirt.

Fuck.

Still. Healing.

"Mmm," she said, stretching for another moment before

shifting to her side and propping her head on her hand. That V gaped . . . and I suddenly had a problem with my shorts fitting properly.

"I need more whiskey," she said.

I started to sit up, reaching for her glass. "I'll go in the house and get you—"

The skies opened up.

Without warning, in that uniquely Southern way. I hadn't noticed the clouds coming in, the already-darkening evening sky hiding their approach.

She gasped.

Then smiled, slow and sexy and plumb full of heat, and reached for the hem of her T-shirt.

"Ava," I warned.

"I think it's a sign, don't you?" she asked, tugging it up, the already sodden material hitting the blanket next to her with a soft *plop*.

I inched back, my fingers itching to touch.

Still. Healing.

As evidenced by the bright red marks on her abdomen.

Her hand went to the button of her shorts.

"*Ava.*"

She flicked it open, tugged down the zipper, and lifted her hips, sliding the material down her thighs.

One slender sexy foot out, leaving the material around the cast.

"Want to help a girl out?" she asked.

I shook my head, too focused on all that skin on display, on those curves. My cock was hard, my mouth was dry, and . . .

She reached behind her, tugged the plain cotton bra up and over her head.

And I stopped thinking.

I closed the distance between us, pulled her on top of me,

and kissed her with every bit of need that had been growing over the last weeks—hell, the last years. My fingers skimmed over the heated silk of her torso, drew patterns in the water dotting her skin. I tugged her down, brought my lips to hers.

"No," she gasped a moment later, pulling back.

Fuck. Too much, too soon. I'd hurt her or scared her or—

I started to set her aside.

She placed her hands on mine, eyes gentle. "No," she said. "I don't want you to love me like I'm fragile, *amore.*"

The endearment made my heart pulse. "How do you want me to love you?"

Her mouth curved. "Like it's our first time and our last. Like you want to hurry up and get to everything and like you want to kiss me inch by inch by inch." She touched my cheek, water streaming down her hair, dripping off her body and onto mine. "Like we only have ten minutes and like we have a century." Her lips came close. "But not like I'm fragile. *Never* like I'm fragile."

My arms closed around her, brought her flush against me. "God, I love you."

Her eyes widened, but since declaring my adoration for this woman hadn't exactly been on my radar, and I wasn't sure if the shock on her face was good or bad, I took her words to heart.

I kissed her.

Like I'd just handed my heart to her on a silver platter.

Because that was what it felt like.

As though she knew what I was feeling, Ava placed her hand on my chest, just over where my heart was thundering. "I love you, too," she murmured, pressing back slightly. "Which is why I think I was so desperate to keep you away. I fell for you a long time ago." Her teeth bit into her bottom lip.

Unsure.

She was unsure and yet so fucking brave. Because she'd let the walls down.

Because she'd let me in.

"I fell for you longer ago."

Amusement replaced nerves. "Yeah? Well, what if I said I fell for you first?"

I nipped her lips. "Should we have a competition to decide who fell in love first?"

A grin. "Maybe."

"Later," I murmured, carefully lifting her off me and setting her on the blanket. A second later, I was on top of her, kissing my way down her throat, nipping at the spot I'd discovered two years ago, just beneath her right collarbone, that was excruciatingly sensitive.

She shivered, fingers tunneling into my hair, holding me close. "You remembered."

"I remember everything."

Just as I'd remember every moment of this day. Love in her eyes, pink on her cheeks. Rivulets of water streaming down those delicious curves. Whiskey on her tongue. Goose bumps on her skin as I kissed my way between her thighs, pushed her underwear down her legs. A heel pressing into my spine.

The way she cried out my name when I licked her.

"Oh—" She broke off, hands falling to her sides, head thrown back. "That's—"

"Mmm," I murmured, circling her clit with my tongue, pressing firmly, sinking a finger into the tight wet heat, and keeping the pressure and rhythm consistent as she arched against me, as her hands clenched, as—

She burst into flames, convulsing around my finger.

"Fuck, you're pretty," I said, moving up her body and kissing her lips, coaxing her down with gentle strokes between her legs. My cock was a hard brand in my shorts, certainly obvious, as my clothing was completely soaked through and plastered against my body.

Her hand trailed lazily up and down my back. "It's not fair you're that good at that."

"I think it's very fair," I told her. "I like eating you out."

"Permission granted," she said. "Anytime you want."

I laughed, pressed a kiss to her temple. "I'm going to take—"

She flipped me in an obscenely tricky move, flopping me over onto my back, rising onto her knees as she straddled my hips. "Your ank—"

Her lips found mine, her tongue thrusting into my mouth, her hands slipping beneath the fabric of my T-shirt.

And I never finished my sentence.

Not when she tugged up on the shirt, and I helped her yank it over my head. Not when she reached behind her and unbuttoned my shorts, shifting so she could tug them down enough to free my cock. Not when she put her hand on me and stroked firmly.

Once.

Twice.

Three times.

I groaned, placed my hand over hers, stilling her, lest I embarrass myself.

She rose up, slowly sank down.

Wet heat on the tip of my cock.

The barest thread of sanity laced through me, and I gripped her hips, stopping her downward motion, even though every cell in my body was telling me to yank her down, to press deep inside, to move and move and *move*. "Cond—"

Her fingers pressed over my lips. "IUD." She smiled.

I nipped her fingertips, guided her hips down instead of up.

And . . . fuck that was everything. Tight and wet, hot and deep. Sliding into her until her pelvis rested on mine. She shifted, pressing closer, a moan rumbling up the back of her throat.

"Dan?" she breathed.

"Yes, love."

A ghost of a smile, bending so her lips met mine. When she straightened, she lifted my hands to her hips. "I think I need a little help. This cast—"

I moved.

Using one of her tricks.

Rolling her to her back, pulling out, thrusting in, all while kissing her with every ounce of love I possessed. This wonderful, difficult, smart, beautiful, amazing woman had given me the best gift of my life.

I wasn't going to waste it.

Out and in. Out and in.

Her uninjured leg hitched around my hip, and I took the hint, tilting my pelvis, hitting her at just the right angle. And fuck, but the moan that dropped off her lips was absolutely the best sound on the planet.

Or maybe that was the way she breathed my name when she got close again, fingers digging into my shoulders, hips meeting mine.

Sweat slid down my back, mingling with the rain.

My abs burned like a motherfucker.

An orgasm coiled at the base of my spine, threatened to burst outward.

Closer and closer, dangerously towing that line of an explosion, and then . . . thank fuck, she exploded, pussy clenching, moisture coating my cock.

I thrust once more.

And catapulted over the edge.

Wave after wave of pleasure slid through me, making every muscle tighten for long, glorious moments. I came to who knew how long later, breathing like I'd run a marathon, thankfully having had enough brainpower left to have remembered to brace myself over her.

"I love you," I murmured, pressing a kiss to each of her closed eyelids.

A smile teased up the edges of her mouth. "You're okay, *amore*."

I nipped that curve. "Just okay."

A pat to my back. "Don't worry," she murmured. "We have plenty of time to work on it."

I growled, nibbled at her jaw, her throat.

She giggled.

And I felt like the luckiest man on the planet all over again.

Especially when she slipped her fingers into the hair on my nape and said, "I love you, too."

The rain slowed to a drizzle.

The sun continued its descent.

The heat returned, not enough to drive us inside, but keeping it warm enough that we stayed outside, the rain drying from our bodies. Ava yawned and rested her head on my chest.

"For the record," she said. "That was better than okay."

TWENTY-EIGHT

Central Georgia
Dan's cabin
09:55hrs local time

Ava

LUNA 2.0 WASN'T LUNA.

But she was pretty damned good.

Lighter than her predecessor, but with good range and a reliable scope.

I'd spent the morning on my belly, practicing on targets Dan had set up in a clearing behind the cabin.

And though my ankle was aching, my abdomen sore from the exercise, I'd felt like Luna 2.0 and I had gone on a great first date.

"Here's to many more," I whispered, stretching my neck and getting ready to pack it in for the moment. The sun had risen, bringing with it all the heat and humidity of the day. And while I'd enjoyed the lazy afternoon and evening yesterday, I was stiff, hungry, and ready for a shower.

Snap.

I didn't immediately react, thinking it was Dan coming out to tell me to take a break. The man could be pushy as hell—case in point, pushing through my walls, not to mention the way he'd gotten my stubborn ass to look inward and reconsider what I'd always thought was the only path for my life. But he was also good, and I wasn't stupid enough to not appreciate that he'd fought for me, that he loved me *because* of who I was and what I'd survived, instead of in spite of all that.

And he loved me.

Me.

When I'd spent so much of my life thinking that was impossible.

I loved him.

Another seemingly impossible feat, and yet something that was . . . so fucking easy. Because it felt right and incredible and like every one of the ragged edges inside me was soothed when he was near.

Snap.

I shifted, preparing to call out, knowing he wouldn't be able to see me readily because I'd moved from the center of the clearing into the shade of a tree about forty-five minutes before.

I might have grown up in the heat of Mediterranean summers, but I swore I was going to wither away in these Southern ones.

Smiling, I pushed my glasses up the bridge of my sweaty nose, reached for the scope, readying to unscrew it, to put it into the case beside me—

Snap.

My nape prickled.

Because that was the third noise, the third opportunity for Dan to announce himself.

And he hadn't.

And my instincts were screaming.

I lifted my head slowly, eyes searching, ears open and listening.

Snap.

Closer this time. Close enough that Dan would have certainly announced himself.

Close enough that the person was dangerously close.

Movement at my back had me leaping up, gripping Luna 2.0 tightly as I spun and faced—

Daniel.

"You're supposed to be dead," I said.

"I'm hard to kill." He smirked, crossed his arms, and leaned back against the tree, less than ten feet from me. The man was handsome, I'd give him that. Large biceps, narrow hips, a pretty face with a strong jaw and kissable lips. Too bad he was an absolute fucker.

Still, he was also close, an easy enough target to shoot.

I lifted my rifle.

"You sure you want to do that?" he asked, stretching casually, and I saw the faint pink line on his throat that must have been the result of Laila's knife at the warehouse.

I put my finger on the trigger. "Pretty fucking sure."

"You're not even going to ask where your boy-toy is?"

I had to work not to react, worry for Dan coursing through me. I couldn't think about that, not at the moment, not when I wasn't certain that Daniel had come alone. Because I was fairly certain he hadn't.

"How do you know about this place?" I asked instead of biting.

A shrug. "Property records are easy to trace when you know what to look for." His eyes flicked to the side, the barest amount of movement I barely detected.

But one I detected just in time.

I swiveled on my cast, my ankle protesting the movement.

I was fast enough anyway, dodging the man creeping up behind me, not bothering to consider as I fired off two rounds that hit him right in his chest. He collapsed to the ground, dead before his body hit the dirt, and I spun back, seeing Daniel had taken several steps toward me.

Pointing the barrel of the gun at his crotch, I asked archly, "Are you attached to that part?"

Palms up, he leaned back against the tree again.

"How's that ankle?"

"Fucking fabulous," I snapped. "Why are you here?"

"Turns out that your dear cousin Sergio would like a word with you."

I expanded my senses, certain there were more of the enemy out there. "And you're what? A fucking lapdog?"

Anger on that handsome face. "I've got something important now," he spat.

"Evil on your soul?" I countered.

A slow, sickening smile. "Power," he said, pushing off the tree again. "So much power that you idiots at the agency don't even know what you're missing. Come with me to Sergio, join your family, and fulfill your legacy. We can rule the fucking world if we play our cards right."

"How?" I asked, lifting the gun slightly higher when he took a step toward me. "By trading in people, in innocents?" I shook my head. "I can never do that."

"Can't you?" he asked condescendingly. "Haven't you already perfected that?"

Once the memory might have had my stomach twisting itself into knots, horror at my past actions making me sick. Today, I knew that I hadn't forgiven myself, but I also knew I wasn't that child of the Toscalos any longer, hadn't been one of them for a very long time.

And I wouldn't ever be again.

A shift in the air to my right, to my left, behind me.

Surrounded.

Fuck.

Where was Dan?

In front of me, Daniel smiled, and I watched him almost from outside my body, sensing his nod almost before he completed it.

Air moved.

I dropped to my knees, out of reach of the first man who came for me.

Pop. Pop.

Dead.

I rolled, spun around, aimed at the one on the other side.

But the cast made me slow, a little clumsy, and it took three bullets to bring him down. I started to push up, but before I could move again, shift to hit the final man bursting through the trees, a hand grabbed my hair, yanking my head back, pain exploding in my scalp.

Daniel grabbed Luna 2.0 and tossed her to the side.

"Enough," he muttered when I threw an elbow, clawed at his hand, kicked back with my good foot. "I said, *enough.*" He punched me hard in the temple, making my vision blacken for a moment, my breath come in rapid gusts.

"Fuck you!" I snapped, throwing my head back, cracking my skull against his chin.

He cursed, fingers loosening, and I ripped myself from his grip, losing more than a few hairs in the process, but then I was free, lurching toward my gun just in time to see Dan burst through the trees and launch himself at the final man who'd tried to come up behind me.

Knowing the man was fucked, I turned back to Daniel.

Only to watch him take off through the trees. Rolling, I propped myself on my elbows, lined up my shot, and . . . fired.

Missed.

I breathed, shot again.

He tripped and the bullet went wide.

"Come on," I whispered, knowing this was my last shot, that if I didn't take him down with this bullet, he would disappear again and—

I pulled the trigger.

Daniel fell.

Then got back up.

"Fuck," I hissed, tossing down the gun, pushing to my feet, determined to go after him, cast on my foot or not.

I turned to check on Dan, saw he'd taken down the final man.

And . . . was clutching his side.

Red soaking through his white T-shirt.

His blue eyes met mine, hazy with pain. "I'm really fucking tired of getting shot," he muttered.

Then he toppled forward.

EPILOGUE

PART ONE

KTS Satellite Base
Western Georgia
16:12hrs local time

Dan

BRIT WAS GOING to kill me.

Three bullet wounds in a month.

Olive glared down at me. "You made me fly from England all the way to this hot-ass hellhole in the middle of the summer. What the fuck is wrong with you?" she snapped.

"I didn't exactly plan on getting shot," I muttered.

"Hmph."

"And you didn't have to fly out here," I pointed out. "Linc had it perfectly in hand."

Her hand covered my mouth. "Do *not* speak the Evil One's name."

I rolled my eyes, the rivalry between the two doctors was well-known, but I didn't say anything further. The woman was checking my wound, I wasn't about to do anything to piss her off.

"The stitches look fine," she grumbled. "Not perfect. But they'll work."

"Such ringing compliments," the Evil One himself said, walking through the door to the infirmary.

Frankly, I considered myself lucky that Lincoln had been here when Ava had driven me in. He was one of the few doctors I trusted, and I'd worked with him before, knew him to be quick and efficient.

And slightly less dramatic than Olive.

Not that I didn't love the girl.

Especially since she slapped the bandage on my side and immediately went to Linc—well, to Ava since Linc hadn't actually just walked through the door. He'd been pushing the wheelchair with *my* girl.

Olive fussed over her new cast, the other having been cut off and replaced when X-rays showed that Ava's ankle was a little worse for wear after her field shenanigans.

I turned to Laila and Ryker, who were parked on my other side. "Any sign of Daniel?"

Laila shook her head. "No. Blood on the ground, but no body."

"Fucker's got nine lives," Ryker said, derision in every syllable.

"Unfortunately, that's true."

We all sat in silence for a heartbeat, and I for one, was wondering when in the hell we'd finally be rid of Daniel. He was the proverbial thorn in our side—no, more than that. He was dangerous, and every minute he lived meant KTS agents were in danger.

Laila clapped me lightly on the shoulder. "I'll save those two from snapping at each other." A squeeze. "I'm glad you're okay."

I covered her hand. "No bullets for a while. Promise."

Her lips turned up. "Better keep that one," she said and walked over to Olive, slipping her hand through the other woman's arm and all but dragging her from the room.

Ryker shook my hand. "Glad you're good, brother."

"Thanks, man."

Then he was gone, following Laila and Olive out the door, looping Linc into conversation, and leaving me and Ava alone.

She wheeled herself over to the bed. "We've got to stop meeting like this."

I snorted, laughter bubbling up, before I groaned and held a hand over my bandage. "Too soon for laughing."

"Sorry." She lifted herself up and out of the chair, sat on the bed. "You okay?"

"Fine, sweet cheeks." I touched her temple lightly, noted a bruise spreading out on the delicate skin surrounding her eye. "*You* okay?"

She made a face. "Not sweet cheeks," she said then pointed at her foot, scowl growing darker. "And it's okay so much as I've got six more weeks in this fucking piece of fiberglass."

"Funny that," I said. "Olive just ordered *me* off for six weeks."

Her eyes brightened. "Yeah?"

"Yup." I tugged a strand of her hair. "More lazy summer days with whiskey and peaches and lemonade?"

She shuddered. "God no," she said. "As much as I've enjoyed our time there, I think that cabin is cursed."

Since she had a point, I simply nodded. "So, what are two agents to do with all this time off?" I asked, rubbing the piece of her hair between thumb and forefinger, soaking in the fruity smell, so fucking glad she was okay, that *I* was alive and able to just be with this woman.

"Six weeks is a really long time."

"An eternity."

Her eyes met mine, a little shy and a lot hopeful. "The start of a future."

"No," I murmured. "The *continuation* of a future. Because," I said when her brows drew down, confusion filling her expression, "start implies an end, and I don't ever want there to be an end with you, Ava. I love you so fiercely, it's engraved on my soul."

Lips parting, breath catching, she shook her head. "Had to get me with the pretty words, didn't you?"

"Every once in a while," I said lightly.

She wiped her eye and laughed, held up her finger, glittering with the moisture of her tears. "This is *your* fault," she said. "You know that, right? Reducing a respectable agent to a blubbering mess."

"Come here," I said, extending a hand and helping her crawl up next to me.

And then because we were both hurting, I kissed her gently.

And then because Ava was my undoing in nearly every way, I kissed her as fiercely as that love in my heart, my soul.

Eventually, she pulled back, touched my cheek, and said, "I love you. I never thought it was possible and never hoped to have someone as wonderful as you." A brush of her fingers. "Thank you for tearing down my walls and helping me see that happiness can come, even if I didn't think I was deserving."

I kissed her forehead, tugged her close. "And you say I have the pretty words."

A light laugh, arms wrapping around me.

I held the woman I loved as our pulses slowed, as our breathing steadied, as sleep crept forward.

"We didn't decide where to go on our six weeks," she murmured just as I was about to succumb to oblivion.

"Mmm," I said, pulling her closer. "You choose this time."

A pause and I swear I felt her smile where her head was pressed to my chest. Or maybe it was just some sixth sense telling me mischief was in the air.

"I'm thinking about that old quote," she said. "You know, the coldest winter I've ever had is a summer in—"

"Ava."

"—In San Francisco, one."

"*Ava.*"

"Because I think it's time your sister sees those three new holes you're sporting, don't you?"

I leaned back, bopped her on the nose. "You're evil."

Her face sobered, and I started to apologize, thinking she'd taken that as a comment on her family, but then she spoke, and her words touched me more than anything else could have.

"Your sister is important to you," she said. "I'd like to meet her as . . . me." Teeth nibbling on her lip, but her chin lifting. "Like the woman who loves you."

See?

All the pretty words.

I kissed her, long and with every big feeling this woman invoked in me.

I kissed her, like the continuation of that future we'd talked about.

Then I held her close, ordered her to sleep, and said,

"I guess we're going to San Francisco."

EPILOGUE

PART TWO

KTS Satellite Base
Western Georgia
16:22hrs

Olive

I STRODE DOWN THE HALL.

Okay, maybe I *stomped* down the hall.

Mostly because of the man at my back.

He was absolutely infuriating.

Case in point, him coming up behind me, grabbing my arm, and turning me to face him. I could have jerked away, could have knocked him on his ass, but my biggest weakness as an agent was one that was my best as a doctor.

I didn't like hurting people.

Even when they wanted to hurt me. I would do it if necessary. I *could* do it if the circumstances required—if my life or the life of my fellow agents or the life of an innocent were threatened.

But I really hated it.

Which is why I simply glared up at Linc as he growled, "Those stitches were perfect, and you know it."

They *were* perfect.

Which was even more infuriating.

But I was used to being infuriated by Linc. Since the moment I'd been recruited to KTS—going from M.D. to field medic to secret agent—he'd made it a point to piss me off.

First, as the man who I'd shadowed to learn the ropes at KTS.

Then as a fellow doctor on the committee I worked on in my non-mission time to write policies and procedures, to authorize and vet new treatments and . . . who questioned my every decision. Who pushed and prodded and was generally frustrating, even as I respected his attention to details.

And now, as the annoyance of all annoyances, treating my teammates.

"They were perfectly adequate," I said, shaking him off and moving back down the hall.

"Perfectly ad—" He broke off, shook his head.

If I hurried, I could make it to the airport in time to catch the plane back to England, and be back, reviewing my policies and procedures, before the clock struck midnight.

Like some pathetic version of Cinderella.

Except instead of the pumpkin coach, I had my files.

I pushed through the door that led into the underground garage, punched in my pin code on the panel near the entrance. It slid open to reveal several sets of keys, each would work on the community cars that were parked here and available for KTS use.

This satellite base wasn't large, and it didn't have a built-in airstrip like headquarters, but it wasn't far.

Since the key fobs were interchangeable, I would drive to the airport, park the car and keep the set with me.

Another agent would pick the car up and use it when they flew in.

Like those scooter rentals littering the sidewalk.

Only these were with much nicer—and wholly bulletproof—cars.

And I was thinking about cars and scooters and interchangeable key fobs because I was desperately trying to *not* think about Linc—and the fact that he was behind me, trailing very close, his spicy scent teasing my nose, his heat at my spine.

Or maybe that was my imagination.

Because there was one additional reason why this man drove me crazy.

I wanted him.

So fucking bad.

But . . . I'd given it a shot. I'd worked up my courage. I'd asked him to go on a date with me.

And he'd turned me down.

Flatly. Coldly. Without hesitation.

"No, Olive," he'd snapped when I'd invited him to dinner. His gray eyes stormy and filled with frost. His lush mouth pressed flat. "Not now. Not *ever*."

So here we were. Annoyance.

Snapping at him so I forgot to be hurt.

"Olive—"

He grabbed my arm again. I shook him off. Again. "Don't touch me," I hissed then forced myself to take a breath, to be kind and gracious, like my grandmother had taught me. "Thank you for your work on my teammates."

Gray eyes edged in storm clouds. That mouth not flat but rather plump and tempting. Linc stepped a little closer. "I don't do this for *thank yous*." A beat. "And I know you don't either."

I didn't. But that also didn't matter.

I shrugged, started to step away. "I wanted to talk to you—"

Stopping, I met his eyes. "About what?"

Now, regret slipped into his expression. "About that night. I want you to know that I didn't mean to—"

Oh lord, now he was going to give me some excuse for why he didn't want to date me. How absolutely fucking pathetic. And miserable.

That too.

"It's fine," I told him, lifting the key fob and striding toward the nearest car. "It's for the best anyway—"

"Olive, I wanted—"

"It wouldn't have worked and—"

"Or it wasn't that I *didn't* want you—"

I clicked the button to unlock the car, unable to hear anything else. "I get it, Lincoln," I told him. "Let's just forget it happened."

I yanked open the door.

And the world exploded.

—Crossing The Line March 22nd, 2021

CROSSING THE LINE

Olive and Linc's story is coming March 22, 2021!
Preorder your copy at www.books2read.com/crossingthelineef

KTS

Bad Boyfriend

Bad Blind Date

Bad Wedding

Bad Engagement

Bad Bridesmaid (March 1st, 2021)

KTS Series

ICE (Hurt Anthology, stand alone)

Riding The Edge (December 7th, 2020)

Crossing The Line (March 22nd, 2021)

Love, Action, Camera (all stand alone)

Dotted Line

Action Shot

Close-Up

End Scene

Meet Cute (April 5th, 2021)

Love After Midnight (all stand alone)

Rum and Notes

Virgin Daiquiri

On The Rocks

Sex on the Seats (April 26, 2021)

Life Sucks Series (all stand alone)

Train Wreck

Hot Mess

Dumpster Fire (February 15th, 2021)

Roosevelt Ranch Series (**all stand alone, series complete**)

Disaster at Roosevelt Ranch

Heartbreak at Roosevelt Ranch

Collision at Roosevelt Ranch

Regret at Roosevelt Ranch

Desire at Roosevelt Ranch

Phoenix Series (**read in order**)

Phoenix Rising

Dark Phoenix

Phoenix Freed

Phoenix: LexTal Chronicles (**rereleasing soon, stand alone, Phoenix world**)

From Ashes

In Flames (January 25th, 2021)

To Smoke

Stand Alones

Someday, Maybe (YA)

ABOUT THE AUTHOR

USA Today bestselling author, Elise Faber, loves chocolate, Star Wars, Harry Potter, and hockey (the order depending on the day and how well her team -- the Sharks! -- are playing). She and her husband also play as much hockey as they can squeeze into their schedules, so much so that their typical date night is spent on the ice. Elise changes her hair color more often than some people change their socks, loves sparkly things, and is the mom to two exuberant boys. She lives in Northern California. Connect with her in her Facebook group, the Fabinators or find more information about her books at www.elisefaber.com.

facebook.com/elisefaberauthor
amazon.com/author/elisefaber
bookbub.com/profile/elise-faber
instagram.com/elisefaber
goodreads.com/elisefaber
pinterest.com/elisefaberwrite